The Soldier's
Secret Son

—

Helen Lacey

P9-DCM-350

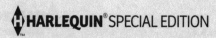
HARLEQUIN® SPECIAL EDITION

Recycling programs
for this product may
not exist in your area.

ISBN-13: 978-1-335-57429-9

The Soldier's Secret Son

Copyright © 2019 by Helen Lacey

Printed in U.S.A.

Helen Lacey grew up reading *Black Beauty* and *Little House on the Prairie*. These childhood classics inspired her to write her first book when she was seven, a story about a girl and her horse. She loves writing for Harlequin Special Edition, where she can create strong heroes with soft hearts and heroines with gumption who get their happily-ever-afters. For more about Helen, visit her website, helenlacey.com.

Visit the Author Profile page
at Harlequin.com for more titles.

Chapter One

Jake Culhane reined in the tall paint gelding he'd been riding for the past two hours and headed for the corral. It had been years since he'd spent so long in the saddle, and his muscles, he was sure, would pay the price later.

It was a chilly afternoon, typical of Cedar River in winter. After living in Sacramento for the last few years, he'd forgotten how cold a South Dakota winter could be. He dismounted by the stables and hitched the horse to the rail, signaling for one of the young ranch hands to take the gelding in the stall.

A few minutes later, Jake headed for the house.

It still felt strange being back. The house, the ranch— all of it held few good memories for him. It was why he'd left at eighteen and joined the army. The truth was, he'd never been much of a cowboy, and the Triple C, one of the largest ranches in the county, needed someone at the helm who had a way with horses and loved the earth and the ranching life. Which wasn't him. The ranch was usually in the safe hands of his elder brother, Mitch. But since Mitch had been seriously injured in an accident several weeks earlier, Jake had stepped up and taken over some of the work around the ranch while his brother recuperated.

Jake circled the house and strode through the back door, wiping his boots on the mat in the mudroom before he made his way into the kitchen. Mrs. Bailey, the housekeeper who'd been on the ranch for close to fifteen years, was working behind the countertop and smiled when he entered the room.

He was just about to snatch a muffin from the plate on the counter when his sister-in-law, Tess, walked into the kitchen from the other door. Despite some initial misgivings about Tess being back at the ranch and his instinctive need to protect his brother, Jake liked her, and was happy that she and Mitch had worked through their relationship troubles and were now back together. Particularly since they had a baby on the way, due to arrive in a couple of months' time.

"Where's the patient?" he asked and half grinned.

Tess smiled. "Living room. And he's grumpy."

"Situation normal then," Jake replied and grabbed the plate Mrs. Bailey held out toward him, piled with a few muffins. "I'll see if this will help."

Jake left the room and walked down the hall, taking a left turn into the front living room.

He spotted his brother by the window, settled in a wheelchair, his broken leg in plaster.

Mitch was two years older, but they had always been good friends as well as brothers. Jake knew the whole family felt grateful Mitch was now recovering from his injuries. It had been a fraught week right after the accident. His younger brother Hank, who was the chief of police in Cedar River, had called him and told him to come home, clearly concerned that Mitch might not make it. Thankfully, his brother had pulled through and was going to make a complete recovery. But it would take some time for him to get back onto his feet. A broken leg, two cracked ribs, countless abrasions and a concussion had almost ended his brother's life. But things were better now. Mitch was back home. He and Tess had reconciled. They were having a baby together. It was a nice happily-ever-after that Jake knew his older brother deserved.

Their own mother had died years ago and their father, Billie-Jack, had bailed. At just eighteen, Mitch had taken custody of sixteen-year-old Jake and the younger kids—fourteen-year-old twins Joss and Hank, twelve-year-old Grant and eight-year-old Ellie. He'd kept them all together and out of family services, something Jake was eternally grateful for. He also knew the sacrifices Mitch had made to keep them together as a family.

"Hey," he said, and placed the plate on the coffee table. "I hear you're in a bad mood."

Mitch turned his head and scowled. "My wife has been telling tales, I see."

Although Tess wasn't technically Mitch's wife yet, their wedding *was* set to take place in the next couple of weeks, and he figured that since his brother and sister-in-law had played loop-de-loop to get their relationship back on track, they could call each other whatever they wanted.

Jake grinned. "Anything I can do?"

Mitch harrumphed. "Get me out of this damned chair and fix my leg so I can get back to work."

"I would if I could," Jake replied and sat down opposite his brother. "But doctor's orders and all that. You need to rest up and heal…no quick fix for that, I'm afraid."

Mitch grumbled under his breath, "Doctors don't know everything."

"Sure they do," Jake said and grabbed a muffin. "You nearly died, remember?"

"I don't need reminding."

"I think you do," Jake said easily. "Otherwise you wouldn't be such a lousy patient."

His brother grumbled some more, then turned his attention to business. "How's the ranch?"

"Running like clockwork. You've got good people here looking after things. Wes knows what he's doing." Wes Collins had been the foreman at the Triple C for a few years and ran a hardworking crew of ranch hands. "And Tess and Ellie are keeping on top of things. All you need to do is rest and recover."

Mitch sighed heavily and ran a hand through his hair. "I know...but it's not easy. And thanks, you know, for staying on and watching over things."

Jake shrugged. "Family first."

"You still moving out today?" Mitch asked and grabbed a muffin.

Jake had been staying at the ranch for the past couple of weeks, but since Mitch was now home and thankfully on the mend, he knew he needed to move and give the soon-to-be-newlyweds some space. Not too far—just into the hotel in town. "That's the plan."

"You don't have to stay at O'Sullivan's," Mitch said quietly. "This is still your home."

"I know," he replied. "But you and Tess need time alone, and I'm not used to being a third wheel."

Mitch laughed. "You're hardly that. And Tess likes having you here as much as I do. Plus, you've always been Mrs. Bailey's favorite."

"That's true," he said and laughed. "Just don't tell Joss."

"He thinks he's everyone's favorite," Mitch said of their younger sibling. Joss owned an auto repair shop in town and was raising his two young daughters alone, as his wife had died many years earlier. "But then, every family has that one standout charmer."

Jake laughed, because Joss *was* actually considered charming—and quite the town flirt. Whereas Mitch was the patriarchal pillar of strength, Chief of Police Hank was the pillar of the community, twenty-eight-year old

Grant was the computer geek and twenty-four-year old Ellie was the baby of the family. And Jake was…what? The bad boy. The war hero. *The one who'd left.* While the rest of his family had stayed in Cedar River and remained together, stayed close, Jake had served two tours in the middle east, moved to California when he retired from the army and begun a business partnership with Trent, a fellow sergeant, working with some of the top tech companies in the state and quickly creating a highly successful security firm.

He been back to Cedar River twice in the last decade. Once for Mitch's first wedding to Tess, and the second time to attend Tom Perkins's funeral. Jake had avoided the town for over six years. Since Tom's death. Since he'd slept with his best friend's widow.

Abby…

His high school girlfriend. Then his ex-girlfriend. Who became his friend's wife.

Shame and guilt pressed down between his shoulders with razor-sharp precision.

"Why O'Sullivan's?" Mitch persisted.

Jake shrugged. "It's the best. And I've become used to creature comforts these past few years."

He knew his brother didn't believe him. "I told you that Abby's working at the restaurant there, didn't I?"

Jake stilled, wondering if Mitch could read his thoughts. Yes, his brother had told him she worked there. He also knew he couldn't avoid her forever. And really, he didn't want to. Which was why he figured he might as well move into the hotel for a while and let fate play its hand. Once, long ago, they'd been friends, and they had both cared about Tom…it was enough of a connection for Jake to want things between them to at least be civil.

"So you said."

"She's an amazing chef," Mitch remarked and bit into a muffin. "I thought she might have left town when Tom's parents moved to Oregon, but she stayed. I guess she wanted to be close to her grandmother."

"I guess," Jake said vaguely. Jake had always liked Mr. and Mrs. Perkins. They were good people and clearly great parents. Jake had spent many nights under their roof after one of his many confrontations with his own father. It was difficult now to think about Tom's grieving parents, about how hard it must have been for them to cope with remaining in the town after they'd lost their only son. He wasn't really surprised they'd moved to Oregon, since their daughter had been living there for many years.

"Abby's got a kid," Mitch said casually. "He's a couple of grades behind Joss's youngest."

Jake had heard Abby had a child. He also knew that she'd remained in Cedar River.

"I'm glad she's happy," Jake said quietly.

Mitch's brows shot up. "I didn't actually say that. Are you still pissed at her for marrying your best friend?"

Jake sucked in a breath. "Abby and I were over long before she married Tom. Whatever we were to one another is well in the past. It's just…history."

"History has a way of repeating itself," Mitch reminded him. "Take it from me… I never would have imagined that Tess and I would be back together. Let alone be about to have a baby."

"You still loved Tess. And she loved you. That's why you're back together. I'm happy for you both…if anyone deserves it, it's you."

"And you?"

Jake shrugged. "Who knows."

"No girlfriend back in Sacramento?"

He shook his head. "No one serious."

The truth was, Jake had spent the last decade without forming one committed relationship. While he was in the military, it had been too hard to maintain something long-distance. And afterward, he hadn't found the time to settle into a relationship. He'd dated several women in the last couple of years, but none seriously. At least, he'd usually broken things off before they became serious. He didn't lie. He didn't cheat. He didn't ever set out to hurt a woman's feelings. He wasn't that guy. He'd simply never felt a connection deep enough with anyone to make it anything significant. The only woman he'd ever loved was Abby…and those feelings had faded long ago.

Maybe he just wasn't a settle-down kind of guy.

"You plan on staying in town a while longer?" Mitch asked.

Jake nodded. "Sure. Maybe another couple of weeks or so."

"I hoped you might hang around until after Christmas," his brother said and shrugged lightly. "I mean, I know you've got a business to get back to, but it's been so good to have you back here. I've missed you."

A familiar guilt wound its way through his blood. Jake knew that Mitch knew he'd never felt at home in Cedar River. And he knew why. His memories were tainted by the last few years he'd spent living on the ranch—by their mother's death, by Billie-Jack's drunken rages, by the car accident that had nearly killed Hank when his brother was fourteen—an accident that had been caused by their father. *And* by his typically angsty teenage relationship with Abby. By the time he was eighteen, Jake had been desperate to get away from Cedar River and everything it stood for.

Until now.

* * *

Abby Perkins ditched the apron she'd been wearing all afternoon, tossed her chef's hat in the laundry tub and made her way out of the kitchen. Her cell beeped in her pocket, and she quickly extracted the phone to check the screen. Her grandmother's text was brief, and she nodded to herself as she headed through to the staff room and opened her locker.

The picture tacked onto the back of the door made her smile. T.J.'s cheeky and infectious grin always put her in a good mood. Even when he was being bad-tempered and defiant, she adored her son and could not imagine a world without him in it. At not yet six years old, he could be a handful, but she was determined not to dampen his spirit and creativity.

Abby pulled on her jacket and tugged the band from her brown hair, hurled it into her locker and grabbed her bag before she shut the door. She caught a glimpse of herself in the mirror by the door and grimaced when she noticed how tired she appeared. It had been a long week. The sous chef had quit…*again*. And two of the waitresses had called in sick. Which meant everyone else was working longer or extra shifts. But Abby loved her job. Being head chef at O'Sullivan's meant she could live with her son in the town she had been born and raised in.

Cedar River, South Dakota, population three thousand and something, sat in the shadow of the Black Hills. Once, it had been a vibrant copper- and silver-mining community. The mines were all closed now, except for a couple that were part of the growing tourist industry. Tourists came through Cedar River on the way to Nebraska and to stay at one of the many dude ranches popping up, or at the luxurious O'Sullivan Hotel. The place was considered one of the best around, and Abby was proud to be a part of that success.

She'd worked at the hotel for a few years. After graduation, she'd scored a position as an apprentice chef at a small restaurant in Rapid City and a year later headed to Paris to study French cuisine for eighteen months. By then, she was already engaged to Tom Perkins, and he had happily accompanied her to Paris. They had spent an idyllic year and a half together in the city—studying, dreaming, seeing the sights. Abby flourished under the guidance of one of the most talented chefs in the city, and Tom had the opportunity to pursue his love of art and music.

When they returned to Cedar River, Abby began working part-time at one of the best restaurants in Rapid City, commuting back to town on the weekends while Tom took a position at the local hardware store. They made wedding plans and bought a house and settled into their life together, marrying two days after her twenty-first birthday.

Four years later, Tom passed away.

Seven months after that, T.J. was born.

And Abby had to make a life for herself and her son.

She'd considered leaving Cedar River many times…to start fresh, to avoid questions and pity and maybe speculation. But her grandmother loved the small town, and other than T.J., she was the only family Abby had to rely on. She supposed she could have moved to Florida to be close to her mother. But her mom had remarried and had her own life, and although she loved her mom and her stepfather was a nice man, Abby had very little in common with her only surviving parent.

So, she stayed in Cedar River.

And waited.

Always on edge. Never truly relaxed. Always wondering, always thinking, always knowing that someday, she would have to face the consequences of that one reckless and unforgettable afternoon.

And it was going to happen soon. She was sure of it.

Because Jake Culhane was back.

Just thinking about him made her insides quake.

She hadn't seen him since two days after Tom's funeral. Which suited her just fine. She didn't *want* to see Jake. But she knew it was inevitable. Cedar River was a small town. At some point, their paths would cross. He'd been back a few weeks, since his brother's accident, and Abby had deliberately kept a low profile, avoiding her usual routine, coming and going from work as discreetly as she could. She'd tried to stay away from the supermarket, the bank, the bakery—anywhere she thought he might show up. But of course, she still had to live her life, still had to run errands to run and things she had to do. She couldn't hide forever.

Thankfully, none of the Culhanes regularly frequented the hotel eateries, as neither family liked the other very much. It wasn't exactly a feud, but since the O'Sullivan and Culhane brothers had gone to the same high school, there was enough testosterone between them to cause a rift that was mainly borne out of a leftover football rivalry.

Abby headed for the staff parking area and within minutes was in her sedan driving from the hotel. She thought about dismissing her grandmother's text message and then changed her mind. T.J. wanted pizza for dinner, and since it was Friday night, she relented and drove directly to JoJo's Pizza Parlor. She scored a parking space outside and switched off the ignition. As always, the restaurant was busy, and she wished she'd called beforehand and placed her order.

Once she was inside, Abby walked toward the counter and waited behind a young couple placing a large order. She looked around, noticing how crowded the restaurant was. All the booth seats were occupied and most of the tables. A couple of women were sitting at the bar, and a few people were seated in the takeout area, clearly waiting for their orders. She fiddled with her car keys as she waited and scanned the restaurant again, catching a glimpse of a group in one of the booths. Four men. All tall and broad shouldered. She recognized the chief of police, Hank Culhane, immediately. And his twin, Joss. The two other men were darker haired. And then dread crawled over her skin when she recognized Jake Culhane's all-too-familiar profile.

His military crew cut was unmissable. His shoulders were exactly as she remembered. His eyes, she knew, were brilliantly green and his jaw strong and uncompromising. He'd always been ridiculously attractive. Since high school. They'd dated for all of senior year, and Abby had been undeniably in love with him. Until he'd broken her heart. Of course, she knew his betrayal wasn't deliberate. But Jake wanted a military career, and Abby had no intention of being the girlfriend—or the wife—of a soldier. She'd watched her own mother go down that path, and it wasn't a life she wanted for herself. So, they broke up, Jake left town and Abby started dating Tom Perkins.

And then, as if on cue, his shoulders tightened, and he turned his head a fraction.

Goose bumps broke out over her skin, and she moved closer to the counter when the couple in front moved to the side, ready to give her order. She quickly selected what she wanted from the menu, paid for the pizza, stuffed the receipt in her purse and was about to head toward the waiting area when she heard an all-too-familiar voice behind her.

"Hello, Abby."

She took a breath, pulled on every ounce of bravado she possessed and turned.

Up close, Jake Culhane was just as gorgeous as she remembered. Six feet two, broad shoulders, the most dazzling green eyes, clean-shaven jaw—he was the perfect picture of masculinity. He was still the most handsome man she'd ever known. The only man who could churn her up inside. The only man who ever made her lose her good sense and reason.

Her ex-boyfriend.

Tom's best friend.

And the father of her son.

"Oh, hey, Jake," she said as casually as she could. "I heard you were back. How's Mitch?"

The whole town knew about the accident that had almost killed his older brother. Thankfully, Mitch had survived, but the event had been serious enough to drag Jake back to the town he hated. She had no idea why he was still hanging around. Jake's visits had always been a few days here or there at the most. In between his tours in Iraq, he'd rarely returned. Now, as he was retired from the military, she had heard he owned some kind of high-tech security business. Not that she cared. She'd stopped caring about Jake a long time ago. But they had history.

And a son.

A child he didn't know was his.

To everyone who knew her, T.J. was Tom's child. Only her grandmother, her mom and her best friend, Renee, knew the truth. Renee lived in Denver, which was where Abby had gone once she'd discovered she was pregnant. She'd needed to clear her head, to grieve for the husband she had lost and work out the next phase in her life. She spent six months with her friend, including the two months after T.J.'s birth. Born nearly seven weeks premature, her son had fought a fierce battle to survive. He'd spent three weeks in the NICU before she could take him home. She returned to Cedar River with a healthy two-month-old baby, and no one questioned his paternity.

Except Tom's parents.

They knew Tom wasn't able to get her pregnant. After two years of trying to have a baby, tests had proven that she would need to pursue a sperm donor if they wanted to have a child. They were considering their options when Tom unexpectedly suffered a severe stroke. He pulled through and for three weeks Abby believed everything would be okay—until another stroke claimed his life.

"He's fine," she heard Jake say, barely able to hear his voice above the screeching going off in her head. "Getting better every day. How are you?"

It was polite conversation. Too polite. The last time they had spoken, it had been heated and unpleasant. A morning-after conversation. A postmortem of the worst kind. Words she never wanted to hear again.

"Great. Never better. You?"

His eyes narrowed fractionally. "Fine. How's your grandmother?"

Gran had always called Jake Abby's quicksand. And she couldn't disagree. When she was seventeen, she had been achingly in love with him. He had been her first real kiss, her first lover.

My last kiss. My last lover.

Her son's face flashed in front of her eyes, and she willed the image away. She didn't want to think about T.J. She didn't want to make comparisons with the man standing in front of her. She didn't want to acknowledge that her son's eyes were exactly the same shade of green, or that they shared an identical birthmark, or that the tiny cleft in his chin was a shadow of the man whose DNA he shared.

Panic clawed at her skin, and she fought every impulse she possessed to run and not look back. And to pretend that nothing was going to change. That Jake would soon leave town and she could feel normal again.

Because it *felt* different.

Ever since she learned he was back, she'd been on edge. Because she knew what was coming—the truth she needed to tell. To Jake and to her son.

"Gran is her usual wonderful self," she replied casually, and willed her food order to hurry up so she could make her getaway. "Still volunteering at the local veterans' home. I hear you left the military?"

"My tour was up," he replied. "It felt like the right time to hang up the combat boots."

Abby didn't want to think about what he'd seen and endured over the course of his tours in Iraq. Her own father had been killed in Desert Storm, and after watching her mother grieve for decades, Abby had been determined she would never get involved with a soldier. Instead, she'd married Tom—safe and dependable—exactly what her young heart had yearned for.

"Well, I'm happy you came back in one piece," she said flippantly.

"I told you I would."

His words had pinpoint accuracy. At eighteen, she'd made her feelings very clear. Terrified he would be injured, or worse, Abby had used his joining the army as an excuse to bail from their teenage romance. Jake had also been clear: he needed to enlist—it was all that mattered.

Not her.

Not them.

And Abby wasn't naive enough to imagine that he'd

changed. Jake didn't have the reputation of a man who hung around. He'd left Cedar River without looking back. He'd left their relationship. And Abby had had every right to forge a new life for herself after he was gone. A life with Tom, because her husband had been a kind and considerate man who had loved her dearly. And he'd stayed by her side, fully supporting her decision to work in Cedar River when she could have had her pick of several of the finest restaurants on the West Coast after returning from Paris.

But Tom knew how important Cedar River was to Abby. Her grandmother had always called it home. Her father and grandfather were buried in the large cemetery at the edge of town. It was a town filled with memory and comfort and the hope for the future. The place where she wanted to raise her son.

But it was also Jake's hometown.

And now that Jake was back, Abby had choices to make.

Tell him...

Don't tell him...

Let him work it out for himself.

It wasn't as though she'd announced to the world that T.J. was Tom's son. She'd simply never been asked to explain why her child looked nothing like her auburn-haired husband. People made assumptions. And Abby was essentially a private person. Too private to be bandying around the details of her personal life.

But she also liked to think she was a truthful person. She was honest in every other aspect of her life. But not when it came to Jake. And now, since everything was different, the truth hovered on the edge of her tongue.

"Jake—" She said his name almost as though it pained her. "I think we should—"

"He'd want us to be friends, you know," he said, cutting her off.

He. Tom. Abby knew how much her husband had liked the man in front of her. Tom had never failed to remind her what a great guy Jake was. About how Jake had stood up for him in high school, protected him from schoolyard bullies, because Tom was a small and sickly and quiet. While Jake was the motorcycle-riding bad boy. They were polar opposites…and yet, they had formed a solid friendship, grounded in trust and mutual respect.

But she knew her time was up. Jake would work it out.

Abby just needed to summon the courage to tell him first.

Chapter Two

"That looked…frosty."

Jake was back at the booth right after Abby had collected her order and left the restaurant. And his brothers couldn't wait to comment on the encounter.

It *had* been an uncomfortable interaction…although not exactly cold. They had too much history to act as though they were strangers to one another. Yet he'd felt the tension emanating from her. But damn, she was still so beautiful. Her brown hair still shone, her pale blue eyes were as mesmerizing as they'd been in high school. Back then, he'd been crazy for her. But it didn't last. Abby freaked out the moment he said he was joining the army. She didn't want to be a soldier's girlfriend. Or wife. They broke up just after graduation.

Jake was already deep into his first boot camp when he'd received a short phone call from Tom, asking if he was okay with his dating Abby. Of course, he was far from okay with whole idea, but there was hardly anything he felt he could really do about it. They were adults. He and Abby were over. And Tom was an honorable guy. True, Jake was pissed for a while, but he got over it. The army, and the front line, were no place for a man haunted by the memory of a girl he'd once cared about. So he wished his friend luck and got on with his life.

And everything was okay for a long time. Until Tom died.

When Jake returned to Cedar River and, for a brief moment, he and Abby found solace in each other's arms.

He shrugged and ignored his brother's jibe. Joss was always the one to speak his mind. Jake had spent so little time with his family in the last decade, sometimes he struggled fitting into the brotherly dynamic that the others clearly shared. Sitting with Joss, Hank and Grant, he could see how close they were.

"It was okay," he replied and drank from the glass in front of him. He'd never been much of a drinker, no doubt due to watching his father drown his sorrows in liquor time and time again. And Jake liked to be in control one hundred percent of the time.

"You're a lousy liar," Joss remarked and grinned. "But this is a small town, so you can't avoid her forever."

"I don't plan on it," he said casually, thinking it was exactly why he intended on staying at O'Sullivan's for a while. "But it was a long time ago, and I don't imagine Abby spares me a thought from one day to the next."

Hank, always the peacemaker, changed the subject. "You staying for the wedding?"

"Of course. Weddings and funerals, that's me." Jake felt bad the moment he said the words, because he *hadn't* returned for Joss's wife's funeral. He'd been unable to take leave at the time, as he'd been deployed on a mission. He looked at his brother. "Sorry, I didn't mean—"

Joss shook his head. "It's okay. We all get it, you know, what you did over there. We know how important it was. I don't imagine it was easy settling back into civilian life."

He shrugged again. His brothers knew some of where he'd been and what he'd done during his two tours. Only some. It wasn't exactly dinner conversation. "I take it day by day."

"We're really proud of you."

Grant's words wrapped around his bones. He wondered how proud they'd be if they knew he'd slept with his best friend's wife two days after the other man's funeral. But perhaps they wouldn't judge. Perhaps they'd understand that his connection to Abby ran deep—deeper than he'd ever been able to admit, even to himself.

When he'd returned to Cedar River a few weeks earlier, he knew he had some bridges to mend with his family. Other than Mitch, he rarely talked to the rest of them. He had a busy life in Sacramento and spent most of his time working. He and his business partner Trent had made a lot of money in a very short time, and they had recently been offered a ridiculously large sum by a competitor who wanted to buy them out. The offer was still on the table, as neither Jake nor Trent was certain they wanted to sell. If they did, he would have to do something else, and he wasn't sure what. Buy a new house? A new car or motorbike? Go on a long vacation? Invest in another business? The truth was, Jake had no real inclination to settle anywhere. He leased a fully furnished condo in Sacramento, drove a top-of-the-range SUV, had more money than he knew what to do with…and carried around an emptiness he wasn't sure he would ever be able to fill. Of course, he thought about the things some of his friends back in Sacramento had—a wife and kids, or at the very least, some kind of committed relationship with another human being.

But…something held him back.

He couldn't work out why he was so reluctant to have a serious relationship. His dating life had been casual. Too casual. The last time he'd spent the entire night with a woman had been six years ago. With Abby. And that had ended up being a disaster.

Tired of thinking about it, Jake bailed on his brothers and headed for the hotel. O'Sullivan's was a boutique-style hotel, with thirty-odd rooms, two restaurants and a bar, and several conference rooms. The place was considered one of the best accommodations in the state. The concierge greeted him and he was quickly checked in. Jake was just about to head to his room when he recognized Kieran O'Sullivan striding across the foyer. Kieran's family owed the hotel—as well as half of the commercial property in Cedar River—and the other man was a doctor on staff at the local hospital. In fact, he'd been on duty the night Mitch had been pulled from the mine shaft accident, and Jake suspected that the reason his brother was alive was because of the man standing in front of him. They weren't exactly friends, but over the years their high school rivalry had dissipated, and now they were friendly enough.

They shook hands, and Kieran spoke first. "How's the patient?"

Jake grinned. "Eager to stop being a patient."

Kieran laughed. "Well, I'm thrilled Mitch's on the mend." He glanced at the swipe card in Jake's hand. "Are you checking in?"

He shrugged. "For a few days."

They chatted for a few minutes about Jake's work and about the hospital, even a little more about Mitch's recovery. When they parted ways and Jake headed for his room, he experienced an odd sense of reconnect. He'd always though Kieran the most reasonable of the O'Sullivans, kind of like how he was sure most people thought Hank was the most likable Culhane. And was very grateful to the other man for saving his brother's life. Plus he liked the idea of not being treated like a complete outsider in town.

He slept like a log that night and awoke the following morning feeling refreshed, which surprised him. Since he'd been back in town his sleep had been mostly restless. He showered, changed into jeans, a long-sleeved shirt and a leather jacket and boots, and then headed downstairs to meet Hank for breakfast in the main restaurant. Out of all his siblings, Hank was the most reasonable and honest, with an abundance of integrity. He was the youngest person to have ever been appointed chief of police, a title he'd held for a few years. Jake respected his brother's strict moral code and the way he'd shown such incredible courage all those years ago, when he'd almost been killed in a car wreck. The ordeal had galvanized them as a family—and had made Jake hate Billie-Jack more than he'd imagined he could hate anyone.

He knew the old man was still alive, knew he lived somewhere in Arizona…but he had no interest in ever reconnecting with his father.

"You paid that speeding fine yet?" Hank reminded him as they were shown to a table and sat down, his brother's six-foot-three frame large enough to block the sun.

Jake had caught a speeding ticket on his motorcycle a week earlier. "Not yet."

"Make sure you do," his brother said. "Don't want to lock you up for unpaid fines."

He grinned. "I'll stop by on Monday. So, what's good here?" he asked and picked up a menu.

"If Abby's cooking," Hank remarked, "everything."

Jake was well acquainted with Abby's cooking. Even before she'd graduated and headed to Paris to study, she had spent hours in the kitchen at the Triple C. He loathed that he tensed at the mere mention of her name.

"You knew she worked here, right?" Hank asked.

He shrugged. "I knew."

"Is that why we're here?" Hank asked and grinned.

"We're here because you said you wanted to catch up," he reminded his brother. "And I happen to be staying right upstairs."

"I thought breakfast would be a good idea," Hank said. "You hardly touched the pizza last night."

A waiter appeared and took their order, and within minutes, coffee was placed in front of them. Jake noticed how everyone acknowledged his brother. Hank possessed a kind of calming, likable aura that drew people in.

"You seeing anyone at the moment?" he asked and sugared his coffee.

Hank shook his head. "Nah. You?"

"Nope. Last I heard I'm afraid of commitment. What's your excuse?"

His brother shrugged. "No time. No woman around here that hasn't tossed me into the friend zone."

"Ouch," he said and grinned. "That's gotta suck."

He didn't hear Hank's reply, because at that moment Abby appeared at a table about twenty feet away and began chatting to the seated patrons. She wore her chef's coat and clogs and was talking and smiling, and the moment she noticed his presence in *her* restaurant was absurdly obvious. Her shoulders tightened, her mouth pressed into a thin line and she met his gaze straight on. Never in his life had he met anyone with such a unique shade of pale blue eyes. He tried not to stare at her or to notice the way her body curved in all the right places. He'd had years to get over his physical reaction to her… ample time to forget the smooth texture of her skin or the sweet taste of her lips. But seeing her brought the memories back with lightning force.

"Are you okay?"

Hank's voice again, drilling into his brain and reminding him what an idiot he was. "I'm fine," he said and dragged his gaze away.

"Still got it bad for her, hmm?"

Jake scowled. "Ancient history."

"I like Abby," Hank remarked.

"You're allowed."

"I think she and Tom were happy. But…"

"But?" He met his brother's gaze. "Your point?"

Hank shrugged. "Tom's gone…that's all I'm saying. And you and Abby are—"

"Nothing to each other," he said, cutting him off.

"So, if I tell you she's on her way over here, that won't even register on your radar?"

His shoulders twitched. "Not at all."

They both knew it was a lie. Seconds later, Abby was standing by the table, arms crossed, clearly trying *not* to look at him.

"Good morning, gentlemen," she said with what was clearly a forced smile.

"Hey, Abby," Hank said easily. "What's good today?"

"Pancakes," she replied. "With bacon and maple butter."

Jake's stomach groaned, and he realized he hadn't really eaten since lunch at the ranch the previous day. He also suspected by the way Abby was deliberately avoiding his gaze that she was burning to put arsenic in his food.

"That sounds good," Hank said and grinned, clearly knowing exactly how uncomfortable Jake was feeling.

"I'll send the waiter back to take your order."

"I was just telling Jake how everything on the menu is good," Hank said so casually that Jake knew something else was coming. "And since Jake is staying at the hotel now, he'll have a chance to try the whole menu."

He saw her stiffen, and her blue eyes darkened. "You're staying here?"

He nodded. "For a while."

"Don't you have to get back to wherever you're from?"

"Sacramento," he supplied and figured she knew exactly where he lived. "And no, not immediately."

He saw something flitter across her face—like uncertainty and fear rolled into one. Which didn't make sense. She had no reason to be afraid of him. They were ancient history. She took a deep breath and spoke. "Well, enjoy your meal. 'Bye, Chief."

Once she was gone and out of hearing range, Hank spoke again.

"Yeah, you were right," he said and grinned broadly. "You two are *nothing* to each other."

"Don't be a jerk."

Hank laughed. "She looked like she either wanted to kiss you or kill you…for your sake, I hope it's the former."

He's staying at my hotel.

Abby wanted to scream. She'd long ago made the decision to *not* be a temperamental chef, so she didn't. But as she charged back into the kitchen, shoulders tight, her head pounding, Abby worked herself up in a frenzy so intense her ribs actually ached.

She didn't want him at the hotel.

It was too…*close*.

She didn't want him eating in her restaurant. Didn't want to see him striding across the foyer, looking so good in his jeans and leather jacket, didn't want to imagine him sleeping in one of the rooms upstairs. The hotel, the restaurant were *her* places. Her haven. Her escape from everything that was linked to Jake Culhane.

It was where she often brought her son on Sundays for breakfast. It was where she worked. Where people knew her. Trusted her. Where no one suspected the truth about T.J.'s paternity because she kept a low profile on her private life. Where she felt *safe* from the truth being discovered. What if he saw T.J.? Jake was a smart guy. It wouldn't take a lot of effort to figure it out.

Damn Jake Culhane.

She pushed some strength into her limbs and got back to work, ignoring the throb in her head and the anxiety churning in her belly.

Abby wasn't sure how she managed to get through the remainder of her shift, but she was relieved when eleven o'clock came and she could swipe out, allowing the other chef to take over lunch. She appreciated that Liam O'Sullivan was a good boss and understood her need to work shorter shifts. This enabled her to also work from home, planning menus, ordering produce, co-ordinating events for the hotel, as well as giving her time with her son, particularly on the weekends. She ditched her whites, grabbed her bag and left through the staff exit. Her car was parked in its reserved space, and she rushed toward the vehicle, stopping abruptly when she spotted Jake leaning on her hood and cursing the personalized plates that made it clear which vehicle was hers.

She stood about ten feet away. "What do you want, Jake?"

"To talk."

She shook her head, wondering, fearing, that he would ask her about her son. *His son.* But why would he? He'd never met T.J. "What about?"

"The past," he quipped and pushed himself off the car. "The present."

God, he was gorgeous. Everything about him was acutely masculine. His broad shoulders, lean waist and hips, long legs, dark hair, and glittering green eyes. Awareness flittered across her skin, and she chastised herself immediately. Thinking Jake was attractive was totally out of the question.

"I think we said everything that needed to be said years ago."

"That was just guilt and regret talking," he reminded her.

But Abby didn't need reminding. She only had to look at her son to remember what they had done and how they had betrayed Tom. The irony was, Abby didn't regret making love with Jake that afternoon so long ago. Because if she did, it would mean she regretted conceiving her son…and a world without T.J. was unthinkable.

She stepped closer, conscious that they were standing in the middle of a parking area and could easily be seen and heard. "I'd rather forget it happened. I wasn't in my right mind. I was grieving and—"

"I know that, Abby," he said, cutting her off. "We were both grieving. I actually wanted to apologize…to say I'm sorry for anything I may have said or done afterward. We both said some things we normally wouldn't have."

Abby remembered. She'd said she hated him and never wanted to see him again. Yes…they had said some harsh and hurtful things that day.

But they had also made a baby.

A baby she'd kept a secret for six years.

"Okay," she said stiffly. "Apology accepted. And I'm sorry, too…for what I said."

Despite the apologies, the tension between them was so thick, she knew he was as skeptical as she was. After a moment, Abby gave a brittle laugh. "Why don't we let each other off the hook, Jake? We don't have to do this. We can leave the past exactly where it is and simply get on with the rest of our lives."

As she said the words, Abby felt like a fraud. Because until Jake knew the truth, she knew she would always be looking over her shoulder. Wondering. Fearing.

"I don't want to be at odds with you, Abby. We were friends once… I'd like to think we could be again."

Friends? Were they? Lovers, certainly. And their relationship in high school had been passionate from the beginning. A complete contrast from her relationship with Tom, which had been grounded in friendship and trust and common ideals. With Jake, it had been hot and angsty and all about passion and sex. Okay…maybe not *all*. There had been times when he was her best friend as well as her lover. And from the way her blood was churning though her veins, some of those feelings lingered still. There was no denying Jake was attractive and sexy as sin.

"Sure," she said casually. "Friends. No problem."

He held out his hand, and after a moment she took it, feeling his long fingers close around hers. It had been years since they'd touched, and a familiar jolt of electric awareness coursed up her arm and landed squarely in her belly. Like always, she was at the mercy of her stupid physical attraction for him. Desperate to get away, Abby pulled her hand free and walked to the driver's side of her car.

"See you around," she said and managed a half smile.

Then she got into her car and drove from the parking area as swiftly as the law allowed.

By the time she got home, Abby was a quivering wreck. She walked up the steps and was greeted by her grandmother at the front door. Moving next door once she returned to Cedar River with her newborn son had been a no-brainer. She'd grown up in Gran's house and loved the leafy, quiet street. Her own home, next door to her grandmothers, wasn't as big. And Gran's had a spacious apartment above the garage that she rented out from time to time, but Abby loved her little house with its large yard and picket fence.

"You look terrible," Patience Reed remarked as she crossed the threshold and walked down the hallway.

"Bad morning," she said, following her. "Where's T.J.?"

"Reading in the living room. He said he wanted to finish the next chapter."

Abby knew her highly intelligent son was also looking to absorb new reading material, so she always had a fresh supply of books for him to read.

"I need coffee," she said and walked into the kitchen.

Her grandmother was close behind her. "Difficult customers?"

"Just one," Abby replied and sank down into a chair. "Jake."

"You saw him again?"

She nodded. "He wants to be 'friends.'" She put quotes around the word with her fingers.

Her grandmother's brows came up. "And what do you want?"

"Part of me wants him to go back to California and leave me in peace," she said honestly. "But that doesn't look likely to happen anytime soon, since he's just checked into the hotel."

"So, he's staying in town?"

"For the moment," she replied and sighed. "I don't understand why, since his brother is out of the hospital and making a full recovery, from what I hear."

Her grandmother's expression narrowed. "Do you think he suspects something?"

Abby shrugged. "I don't know. I don't think so. I mean, I don't see how he could. I don't know, Gran, maybe someone has said something to him and he's hanging around to check it out. I don't know what Jake thinks. I never have. The man is a closed book. I just know that he's staying at the hotel and I'm a nervous wreck."

Patience poured coffee and came around the countertop. "You knew this would happen, Abby. It was always inevitable, considering his family is settled here.

And it's the right time for the truth to come out. We both know that."

"At T.J.'s expense?" She shook her head. "I don't think so."

"I can't imagine Jake would be a threat to his son."

"Don't call him that, Gran," Abby said tightly.

"It's the truth, and the truth needs to be faced. I know you think you've done the right thing by allowing T.J. to believe that Tom is his father, but until you tell him the truth about Jake, it's going to be a lie that you'll have to live with for the rest of your life. And for his."

Shame pushed down on her shoulders. Because her grandmother was right. She had *allowed* T.J. to think Tom was his dad. And she'd never corrected anyone's assumptions about Tom being the father, either. But now, things were very different. Jake's unexpected return had changed everything and she knew her son needed to be emotionally prepared for what was inevitable—meeting his biological father.

"I thought I'd have more time," she admitted.

"You've had six years, Abby."

Her guilt amplified. "I know you're right. In my heart I know Jake has the right to know. And so does T.J. But I'm worried that Jake won't hang around…and where will that leave T.J.?"

Her grandmother regarded her cynically. "Sounds to me like you're looking for excuses to avoid telling Jake what you should have told him when you first discovered you were pregnant."

Patience had always made her disapproval clear, but she had still supported Abby completely. And she knew her grandmother adored T.J.

"I don't know what to do, that's the truth. For all I

know, Jake could pack his bags and leave tomorrow, so I don't see the point in creating chaos unnecessarily."

"Does that mean you're not going to tell him?" her grandmother asked bluntly.

Abby sighed. "No, Gran, it means I'm going to take some time and see how things pan out. If Jake—"

"Proves himself worthy?" her grandmother suggested.

"Something like that."

"Do you think that's fair?"

Abby shrugged. "No…but I have to protect my son, and I will do that at all costs."

Patience nodded agreeably. "I know you want to protect him. But do you think that perhaps you also want to protect yourself?"

Abby feigned ignorance. "I don't know what you—"

Her grandmother held her gaze. "He's always been quicksand for you, Abby. Did you think time would make that go away?"

"I guess I had hoped it would," she replied and took a shuddering breath. "My feelings toward Jake have always been complicated," Abby admitted on a sigh. "But if I tell him, it has to be because it's what's best for T.J."

"You know I support you," Patience said generously. "But you need to tell him the truth, Abby, while you have the opportunity and *before* that opportunity is taken from you."

She knew her grandmother was right.

But the idea still scared her to pieces. She had no idea what Jake's reaction would be. Anger? Disbelief? Or worse…indifference? What if he wanted nothing to do with T.J.? She hoped, deep in her heart, that there was a middle road, some way of Jake knowing the truth without the revelation having any negative impact on T.J.'s life.

Or on mine.

She got to her feet, pulled her cell phone from her bag and called the hotel.

Seconds later she was put through to Jake's room.

"It's Abby."

He was silent for a moment and her knees trembled.

"I'm surprised to hear from you."

Abby took a long breath. "We need to talk, Jake. Can you meet me somewhere?"

She was sure she heard him hesitate. "Ah...sure."

"The Loose Moose, seven o'clock," she said quickly, before she lost her nerve, and then ended the call before she could change her mind.

Chapter Three

Jake had no idea why Abby had done a complete 180.

Only a few hours earlier, she'd regarded him with a kind of wariness that made her opinion abundantly clear—they really had nothing to say to one another.

But as he walked into the Loose Moose, a tavern a few blocks from O'Sullivan's, Jake knew the conversation was far from over. He looked around, scanning the room and patrons. The place had undergone a complete restoration a couple of years back, after a fire had nearly destroyed it. Jake knew the new owner, former army vet Brant Parker. They'd gone to school together, although the other man was a year or so older, and had bumped into each other occasionally over the years. And he remembered that Brant's wife, Lucy, was a friend of Tess's. The tavern was well appointed and family friendly and busy, as expected, for a Saturday evening.

Jake spotted Abby immediately, sitting alone in a booth in the corner, her hands twisting together nervously. Her hair was down and she wore jeans and a long-sleeve shirt and faux fur jacket. He experienced an odd tightening in his chest as he approached her. There was such a great divide between them, a wall built from years of words said, of words unsaid and the guilt of seeking comfort with one another when they had been at their lowest ebb. Jake wasn't a fool—he knew exactly what had happened that afternoon so many years ago. And he knew he was equally to blame for all of it.

He'd turned up at Abby's house to say goodbye, to let her know he was heading back to his post in Iraq. But he wanted to check up on her, to ensure she was okay. He'd expected to find her crying. But she'd been unwaveringly stoic when she answered the door and ushered him inside. He remembered her unhappiness, her vulnerability, the quaver in her voice as they sat and talked. And then, like in a dream, they were kissing. Softly, at first, more for comfort and reassurance, and then things changed and they were both swept up in a passion that still had the power to knock him to his knees. Afterward, there had been regret and recrimination. From both of them.

As he approached the table, she looked up. She wasn't smiling, and Jake was sure he saw uncertainty in her expression. Of course, things were always going to be uncomfortable between them until they sorted through their past. And Jake knew he needed to make amends to the woman who had been his best friend's wife. And the girl he had once cared about.

"Hello," he said quietly and slid into the booth. "It's good to see you again."

"Hi, Jake."

A waitress approached to take their order, and he waited while she requested a club soda. He did the same.

Once the waitress left, Jake spoke again. "I was surprised you called."

She took a long breath. "I thought we should talk."

He nodded. "Me, too. I don't want us to have all this unresolved tension between us, Abby."

"Then what do you want?" she asked calmly. "Why does it matter if there's tension?"

Jake stilled. "Because…we're…"

"What, Jake?" she shot back quickly. "Friends? I don't think we've ever exactly been friends. We dated in high school, we broke up and then I married Tom." She paused for effect. "You were noticeably absent from our wedding."

Jake's insides tightened. He'd just been deployed at the time but hadn't made much of an effort to take leave. Watching his best friend and ex-girlfriend tie the knot had been one of those experiences he could live without.

"I was in—"

"I know," she said, cutting him off. "We knew where you were and what you were doing, and Tom understood. But what happened later…after the funeral…that was a moment of craziness, and no matter how hard I try, I can't simply sweep it under the carpet and pretend it didn't happen. We can't undo the past, Jake."

"I'm not suggesting that we should. I only know that Tom wouldn't want us to be like this."

Her brows shot up. "Do you really think you'd know what my husband would want?"

"We were friends," Jake said quietly.

"He worshipped you," she said and crossed her arms. "And made excuses for you. He always said you would never come back to Cedar River for good. Is that true?"

Jake frowned. An inquisition wasn't what he expected. "I have a life in Sacramento. A business. Friends."

"Girlfriend?" she inquired quietly.

The waitress returned with their drinks, and once she was gone, Jake replied. "No."

"You've never married?"

"Is that a question, or a statement?"

She shrugged. "A little of both. But I'm curious… you've been a civilian for a couple of years now. Why haven't you settled down?"

Jake's uneasiness increased. He wasn't used to discussing his personal life. "Why haven't you?" he shot back, diverting her question. "I mean, why haven't you married again?"

She took a sip of her drink. "I've been busy with work and my—"

"Son?"

She met his gaze, and her eyes widened fractionally. "Yes. T.J."

Tomas John? Named after his father. It was cute, he supposed. Tom would have liked the idea. His friend was a big believer in family and putting down roots. And Jake knew would have made a great dad, had he been given the chance. Jake had never given the idea of fatherhood much thought. He hadn't exactly had a great role model in his own parent. And since the army, the notion of settling down, of being in one place, didn't sit right. Even Sacramento mostly felt temporary.

"Your son is, what? Six?"

"Almost. He turns six in March."

Jake did a vague mental calculation, in an abstract kind of way. She'd borne Tom's son. And he was happy for her that she had a child to honor the memory of the man she had loved. A man who had often helped Jake through the toughest part of his life with his kindness and understanding.

"Is he like his father?"

She took a drink and then swallowed. "Yes, very much so."

Jake drank some soda and sat back in the seat. "I'm surprised Tom's parents left town. I mean, I know their daughter lives in Oregon, but I thought they would have stayed here to be close to their grandson."

She shrugged. "They wanted to be somewhere where

they weren't constantly reminded of their son. People leave for all kinds of reasons—you should know that."

It was a direct hit. "You know why I left, Abby."

"Because you wanted the army more than you wanted anything else," she said quietly. "I remember my mother saying my father had thought the same thing. I am curious why you've stayed away, though. I mean, your whole family is here, and the ranch. I would have thought those reasons alone might have made you want to come home permanently."

Home? Strange, but Jake had never felt as though anywhere truly fitted that description.

He shrugged loosely. "The ranch belongs to Mitch, and now that he and Tess are back together and having a baby, they can start a new legacy, a new generation. I'm sure they'll do a much better job than the old man ever did."

Her gaze narrowed farther. "I take it you haven't reconnected with your father?"

"Hell, no. I never want to see him again. What about you?" he asked, figuring he was owed a couple of questions. "You see your mom much?"

Abby shook her head. "Not really. We talk on the phone, of course. She married a nice man called Clive and lives in Florida. I usually go with Gran and visit her for Christmas if I'm not scheduled to work. She never really liked South Dakota and you know I was always closer to Gran than my mother. This was my father's hometown, not hers. In a way, even though she grieved him for so long, I think she was glad to meet someone else and get away from here."

Jake wondered if Abby might do the same, so he asked her, "Do you think you'll get married again?"

She looked at him oddly. "I'm not sure. I'd like to have more children at some point."

"I bet you're a good mom."

She half smiled—the first time she'd looked anything other than disapproving since he'd sat down. "I'd like to think so. I'm sure T.J. would disagree with me when he's failing to get his own way."

Jake grinned and then looked at her soberly. "I don't imagine it's easy doing it on your own. My brother Joss juggles the whole single-parent thing like a pro, although I'm not sure how he does it."

"If he's anything like me, smoke and mirrors," she said lightly. "And I'm lucky I have my grandmother to help. I bought the house next door to hers."

"Does she still live on Vale Street?"

Abby nodded. "Yes."

He remembered her grandmother's house very well. They'd spent a load of time in Abby's bedroom when they were dating, mostly on the pretense of studying. But they'd shared a lot of make-out sessions in her room. In fact, they'd lost their virginity together on her narrow bed with its pale mauve coverlet.

Jake noticed that Abby's gaze had dropped a fraction, and he wondered if she was remembering the same thing. "I know this is going to sound crazy, Abby—but I'd like us to clear the air. You know, lay it all out and start fresh."

She looked skeptical. "Why?"

Jake sighed. "Because it feels like we should."

She didn't say anything for a moment. But she looked at him. Into him. In a way that stirred up a whole lot of memory. And something else—a familiar feeling of awareness, as though for that moment, they were the only two people on the planet. During their relationship they had experienced varying and conflicting emotions—love, lust, resentment, anger, despair, resolution—all of them bound by a connection that went deeper than the transparent interaction they were now having. And Jake knew she was as aware of it as he was.

"Okay," she said quietly. "We can leave the past exactly where it is and start over. Now that's settled, you can leave town with a clear conscience."

Jake watched as she fiddled with the paper napkin in her hand, as though she was filled with a kind of restless and nervous energy. He couldn't fathom her. She'd called him, after all. Jake wasn't under any illusions in regard to Abby's feelings about him. But he was curious about why she'd agreed to meet up when she clearly wanted to be somewhere else.

He raised his glass and met her gaze. "Who says I'm leaving?"

Abby was a nervous wreck. Her spine was rigid, and she could barely stop her hands from shaking.

Just tell him...

But she couldn't. The words wouldn't come out.

And now that he'd made some casual comment about *not* leaving town, she was more confused than ever. She stared at him, examining every angle of his handsome face, looking for some indication that he was suspicious about T.J.'s paternity, and found nothing.

"You're not?" she queried.

He shrugged his gorgeous shoulders. "Not immediately. My brother is still recuperating, and I need to spend some time with my family."

Abby's insides clenched. "So, how long?"

"How long am I staying?" He shrugged. "I'm not sure. A few weeks. A couple of months, maybe. There's no real urgency for me to get back. My business partner has the company well under control."

She'd heard rumors about how successful his business

had become in a few short years. Jake was a highly intelligent man and she wasn't surprised that he'd carved out a great career. In high school he hadn't had to work hard to get good grades, and she recalled he was something of a math whiz.

Like his son.

She shook off a stray chill and refocused on the conversation. "You're rich, I suppose?"

He chuckled. "I do okay."

"Tell me about your business."

He shrugged a little uncomfortably. "It's a security firm. The software kind, not armed guards. High-rises, shopping malls, theme parks, big hotels…that kind of thing."

"Do you travel a lot?"

"Not really," he replied. "My partner is more the face of the business. I'm more behind the scenes, doing the tech stuff."

"You didn't want a longer career in the army?"

He half shrugged. "I considered it. But by the time I'd made the rank of sergeant I knew I wasn't made to be a career soldier."

"So, why Sacramento?" she asked.

"No reason…just where I ended up after I retired from the army. My buddy had family there and a few connections, and so we started the business and in a couple of years we were on our way. It's a nice enough town."

He didn't seem particularly connected to the place where he worked and lived. Unlike Abby, who had a deep-rooted love and connection to Cedar River. Even Paris hadn't been enough to convince her that there was a better place in the world.

"Just a place to hang your hat then?"

He shrugged. "I guess…for now." A waitress passed

their table carrying a tray piled high with ribs and buffalo wings, and he glanced back to Abby. "Want to have dinner? The food actually looks really good."

She shook her head. "This isn't a date, Jake. In fact, I should probably get going. Thank you for meeting me."

"Did it help, to get you to stop hating me?"

She stilled in her seat. "I don't hate you."

He raised a brow. "No? Just giving a good impression of it then?"

Abby swallowed hard. "It's not hate. It's…humiliation. And embarrassment. And guilt. All the things I know are wasted emotions…but I still can't help feeling them. Betraying someone who loved you is a hard pill to swallow. And yes," she said and waved a hand loosely. "I know Tom was gone and we weren't *actually* betraying him…but it feels like we did, in here," she said and briefly touched her chest. "It's not logical. But feelings rarely are."

"So, what would you like me to do? Say I'm sorry?" He shrugged a little. "Okay, I'm sorry. Really, I am. I never meant to hurt you, Abby."

Abby wanted to say the same words back to him. But in her heart, she couldn't be sorry for what happened between them. Because that would be like admitting she was sorry that T.J. had been conceived, which was unthinkable.

She grabbed her bag and slid from the seat. "Good night, Jake."

He met her gaze. "Can I see you again?"

Every instinct told her to scream a resounding *no*. But she couldn't avoid it. So, she nodded vaguely. "Sure, let's catch up soon."

She didn't wait for a reply and then quickly left the Loose Moose. Arriving home fifteen minutes later, she found her grandmother sitting in her front living room, watching television. It was close to nine o'clock, so she knew her son would be asleep. Patience immediately flicked off the volume and waited while Abby dropped into the sofa.

"So, how did it go?" her grandmother asked.

Abby stretched out her legs. "It was fine."

"Did you tell him about T.J.?"

She shook her head quickly. "Of course not. I wanted to talk to him, find out what his plans are."

"Gathering intel?"

She shrugged. "Something like that. He's says he's staying in town for a while longer."

Patience gave her an inquiring look. "Isn't that what you wanted?"

Abby had no idea what she wanted when it came to Jake. "I want to make sure I protect my son. Thank you for watching him tonight, Gran. I don't know what I would do without you."

After her grandmother went home, Abby stayed in the living room for a while and stared at the empty corner near the window, a spot that was waiting for the Christmas tree. Now that Thanksgiving was over, the holiday season was looming. T.J. adored Christmas. He was in the upcoming pageant at school, and Abby had been volunteering on the costume committee. The sense of community and inclusion was one of the things she loved most about Cedar River.

She yawned, stretched, walked around the house turning off lights and then headed to T.J.'s room. Her son was fast asleep, clutching his favorite stuffed dragon toy, one arm flung out of the covers. She tucked the comforter around him and gently kissed his forehead. A surge of love washed over her like a warm and familiar wave. The intensity of her feelings for her child was simply boundless. He was her sun and moon, her night and day, a bond that had formed the moment she knew she was pregnant.

Looking at him now, seeing his dark hair tousled over his forehead and the soft curl of his mouth, Abby saw Jake in every angle of his small face. Love quickly merged with guilt and regret, and she sucked in a shuddering breath.

Gran was right. Her son deserved to know his father. His *real* father.

Abby knew she had to tell both T.J. and Jake the complete truth…not an abridged version. Only, she wasn't sure how.

She flicked off the night-light, left the door ajar and walked down the hall to her own room. Once she had showered and changed into her warmest pajamas, Abby slipped into bed. Restless, she lay awake, staring out of the window. There was enough light visible through the gossamer curtains to see a few stars. It was cold outside, but the sky was clear. Snow was forecast, but Abby didn't mind. She enjoyed the opportunity to spend time with her son in the snow. He'd been pleading for a snowboard for months, but she hadn't overcome her overprotective instincts quite yet.

She knew he'd inherited that adventurous gene from Jake. Her ex-boyfriend had been well-known for his thrill-seeking antics when he was young. From skiing in the winter months to riding his motorbike up the winding roads along Kegg's Mountain, Jake Culhane had always had adventure in his blood. Which was probably why the army had called to him so strongly. Of course, she knew part of it was to get away from the memory of his violent father. But she believed a part of it was the idea of being overseas and seeing the world. Where Abby was the complete opposite—even when she was in Paris with Tom, the call of home always beckoned.

Abby closed her eyes, willing herself to go to sleep. But, as always of late, her dreams made her uneasy, and she awoke feeling lethargic and edgy. She rolled over as the sun peeked through the curtains and opened her eyes, smiling when she spotted T.J. sitting on the edge of her bed, his concentration solely on the book he held in his hands. It was a Sunday morning ritual when she didn't have to work—he would bring a book into her room, and they would read together for a while, then head into town to have breakfast.

"Good morning, Mommy!" he announced when he saw she was awake. "I brought my favorite one today," he said and waved the book. "The one about the dinosaurs."

Abby laughed and hugged him, ruffling his hair, inhaling the little-boy scent she loved so much. They read for a while and then got dressed, heading out around eight thirty.

"So, what do you feel like for breakfast?" she asked as they headed into town.

"Pancakes," he replied quickly. "Or waffles."

Abby chuckled. "You say that every time."

"'Cause they're my favorite, Mommy," he said and grinned.

She nodded. "I know. So, where would you like to go? The bakery or O'Sullivan's?"

"Great-Grandma's," he said and giggled. "She makes the bestest pancakes. Except for yours, Mommy."

That was true. Patience was a wonderful cook. It was from her grandmother that Abby had developed her own passion for cooking.

"You know that when I'm not working that Sunday is our special day together. And Grandma has plans this morning, so it's just us."

T.J. nodded and giggled again. "You pick, Mommy."

Thinking she would give O'Sullivan's a wide berth because of a certain hotel guest, Abby drove through town and scored a parking space outside the bakery, pulling up beside a shiny hog. They served both pancakes and waffles at the bakery, and she knew the place was child friendly. She got out and opened the back door to help her son from his seat, locked the car and headed inside.

As soon as she entered the bakery, she spotted a friend, Annie Jamison, sitting alone at one of the tables. The other woman looked up and waved, beckoning them over. Annie was a nanny who worked for David McCall, a widower who happened to be Jake Culhane's cousin. And Annie's stepsister was Tess Culhane. Cedar River certainly was a close-knit community and Abby marveled over the fact that no one had worked out who T.J.'s father actually was. Particularly since T.J. looked nothing like Tom—who'd had auburn hair and freckles and pale skin. T.J. had inherited Jake's coloring and his green eyes.

And the lightning-bolt birthmark on his shoulder.

"You look tired," Annie said to her and grinned as T.J. scrambled into a seat.

"It's been a long week. What about you? Taking the day off?"

Annie shrugged. "David's taking the kids to Rapid City, so I thought I would take some much needed *me* time."

Abby nodded. She knew her friend had her own troubles. "Are you still thinking about quitting?"

Annie half nodded. "Thinking, yes. Deciding…no."

"Mommy." T.J.'s voice broke in between them. "I'm *starving*."

Abby chuckled at his dramatic tone and dug into her bag for her wallet. When she didn't find it, she remembered she'd left it in the console in the car. "Can you watch him for a minute?" she asked her friend and explained.

She was just locking the car door, having grabbed her wallet and stuck it into her bag, when she heard her name being spoken from behind. Turning quickly, she saw Jake standing on the sidewalk, dressed in jeans, cowboy boots, a white shirt and leather jacket, a motorcycle helmet in his hand.

"Oh, hi there," she said nervously, spotting T.J. through the window and wishing she'd gone to O'Sullivan's instead per their usual habit. She glanced at the motorbike parked nearby. "Yours?"

He nodded. "You look nice."

Abby glanced down at her beige cargo pants, long-sleeve red T-shirt, scarf and woolen jacket and remembered how she'd thrown the outfit together without much thought. She managed a tight smile and nodded. "Thanks. Well, I should get going."

"Me, too," he said quietly. "I only stopped here for coffee."

He was going into the bakery.

No. Abby's heart nearly stopped.

Not yet… I'm not ready for this yet.

"You know the coffee at the hotel is good."

"I know," he replied. "I had some with breakfast."

"Oh…okay. Well, the café down the block also does a great brew."

His mouth twisted, and he jerked a thumb in the direction of the bakery. "Something wrong with the coffee here?"

Abby's heart thundered in her chest. "Ah…no… I just…"

"After you," he said and waved his arm in an arc, indicating for her to walk ahead.

Abby took a long breath, galvanized her knees into

Chapter Four

Jake wasn't sure what he thought as the small boy raced toward Abby and grabbed her hand. He was a nice-looking kid. Dark haired, like his mother. He stared at the child for a moment, searching for something of his friend in the boy's features, and didn't find anything of Tom in the child's expression. Obviously the child took after Abby.

"Mommy, Mommy," he chanted and tugged her hand. "I'm hungry."

"Okay," she said breathlessly. "What would you like? Pancakes? Waffles?"

The child bit his lip, tilted his head and then looked directly at Jake. "Who's that?"

Jake heard Abby suck in a sharp breath and then waved her hand. "This is a…friend. His name is Jake."

The boy held out his hand in a grown-up manner and introduced himself. "I'm T.J."

Jake took the child's hand and shook it gently. Strange, he thought as he held on, how meeting Abby's son made something uncurl in his chest. An odd feeling of familiarity that was warm and welcoming. *Because he's Abby and Tom's child.* He shook the feeling off, let go of the boy's hand and spoke.

"It's nice to meet you. T.J. So, you said you were hungry. Do you come here a lot? What's the best thing you've had here?"

"Muffins," the kid said swiftly and laughed. "And waffles. And pancakes. And cinnamon rolls. Except I don't really like cinnamon."

"Me, either," Jake admitted and smiled, thinking that the child was smart and articulate for his age.

"I just like the sugar on top," T.J. said and grinned, exposing one missing tooth at the front.

"Me, too," Jake replied.

"Mommy, can I have pancakes?" the child asked politely.

Jake glanced at Abby and realized that she looked ghostly white, almost unwell. Her eyes were as large as saucers, and she inhaled sharply. He met her gaze, surprised by her sudden paleness.

"Are you okay?" he asked.

She nodded. "Fine…just fine. It's been a long week at work."

"Temperamental chefs?" he queried and grinned.

"Something like that."

"Mommy," her son said again and tugged on her hand. "Pancakes?"

"Of course," she said quietly. "Pancakes."

Jake wasn't entirely convinced that she was okay, but he nodded agreeably and waited while she ordered food for her son and tea for herself.

"Is Jake sitting with us?" her son asked cheerfully.

Jake saw her expression immediately flatten. "Ah… I don't—"

"Sure," he said and nodded. "If your mom doesn't mind?"

"Can he, Mommy? Please."

She hesitated a second and then waved a hand. "Of course."

He quickly ordered coffee and passed the shop clerk a couple of bills, paying for both orders.

Jake waited for Abby to protest, to tell him she could certainly pay for her own meal…but she didn't. She muttered a barely audible thank-you and turned.

"That's our seat," T.J. said and pointed across the room to a table in the corner.

Jake spotted a woman he recognized already sitting at the table. Annie Jamison. He waved absently, and she smiled in recognition. Moments later, they were all seated at the table.

"How's everything with you, Jake?" Annie asked, both brows up.

"Good. You?"

"The same."

It was harmless small talk, but Jake was aware of how tense Abby was sitting to his left as Annie and T.J. chatted intermittently. Her hands were clenched tightly in her lap, and her mouth was pressed into a thin line. She looked as though she longed to be somewhere else. And Jake knew he was the cause of her discomfort. Despite their fragile truce, he wasn't fooled. Abby wanted nothing to do with him.

"How's Mitch doing?" Annie asked and smiled.

"Better," he replied and nodded. "But he's a terrible patient. Very grumpy."

T.J. giggled and was then instantly distracted when the waitress brought his juice and their drinks to the table. The woman, who was in her midtwenties, was very pretty and had bright blue eyes, and she passed Jake a look he recognized instantly. In another time, and another place, he might have looked in return. He might had offered her a welcoming smile and maybe asked for her number. But he wasn't in Cedar River to hook up or get laid. He'd come back to be with his family, to support Mitch while he recuperated. And maybe to make amends with Abby. He wasn't sure why it was important. They weren't friends. They weren't anything to each other. But over the past few years, he'd realized that he'd never truly have peace of mind until he'd doused the flames on the bridges he'd burned. And Abby was at the top of the list.

"How long are you planning on staying in town?" Annie asked.

Jake flicked his gaze toward Abby for a moment. "I'm not sure." He noticed how Abby's hands were still twisting in her lap and her mouth remained tight around the edges. "A few weeks, I guess, until Mitch is back on his feet. Your sister is doing a great job helping him recuperate."

Annie smiled. "We're all very happy that Mitch and Tess have found their way back to one another."

"It's been a long time coming," he said quietly. "It's good they're making it work, for the baby's sake."

"They love each other," she said and shrugged lightly. "They just needed to remember that."

Jake didn't disagree. Mitch and Tess certainly were deeply in love. In a way, he envied them. Despite every obstacle, they had worked through their past differences and the hurt and managed to find a way to be together. It almost made Jake believe that happily-ever-afters were possible.

Annie nodded, grabbed her coffee and then got to her feet. "Well, I have to run, I promised Tess I'd catch up with her this morning. Good seeing you, Jake." She said farewell to Abby and T.J. and left the café.

Once she was gone, Jake sipped his coffee and tried to ignore the uncomfortable silence. Well, the silence from Abby—her son was chatting nonstop about school and snowboarding and his favorite Marvel hero. He seemed like a smart kid, and quite social for his age, Jake realized. It made him think how proud Tom would have been to know his child was happy and healthy. Tom would have made a great dad. He was the kind of man who was incredibly likable—considerate and sincere, loyal and trusting and the best kind of friend.

Not like me...

Jake had been filled with his own kind of self-disgust for years.

And guilt.

Which, he figured, Abby was feeling, too, right about now.

"Mommy won't let me get a snowboard," T.J. announced and then looked sulky.

Jake bit back a grin. "She won't?"

The boy shook his head and frowned. "She says I might *perjure* myself."

"Perjure?" he echoed and glanced at Abby.

She made a face. "I said *injure*. Snowboarding is dangerous."

"So is walking across the street," Jake remarked quietly, ensuring her son couldn't hear him, and then raised a brow.

"That's the expected response from an adrenaline junkie," she muttered.

Jake laughed. "Is that a dig?"

She shrugged and passed her son a paper napkin. "An observation."

Jake drank some coffee. "For the record, I don't have any dangerous pastimes these days."

"What about your motorbike outside"

His mouth twitched. "Simply a mode of transport."

"And the speeding ticket you got the other day?"

He frowned. "You know about that?"

"There are no secrets in a small town."

Jake held her gaze. "No?"

She shook her head and stirred her tea, clearly not wanting to look in his direction. Jake noticed that T.J. was biting his lower lip, the same habit his mother had. It was cute, and the more he saw them together, the more he realized the boy looked nothing like Tom.

"I'm never getting a snowboard," T.J. said sulkily.

"That's not what I said," Abby replied. "I said one day, when you're older. It's not simply a matter of getting a board. There's also the fact you'll need lessons and I—"

"I'll teach him," Jake said quickly and realized immediately he'd said the wrong thing, because Abby was glaring at him. "I mean, if you want. I know you don't ski so—"

"I ski," she said defensively. "I just have a problem with—"

"Balance," he said and grinned. "I know. Remember when I tried to teach you how to ride a horse?"

She scowled. "I'm scared of horses."

"I wanna ride a horse!" T.J.'s voice rang out between them. "But Mommy won't let me do that, either. I never can do anything."

She made an impatient sound, took a breath, and then her expression softened a little. "Please don't encourage him to be reckless. I just want him to stay safe."

"I'm sorry," he said quietly. "That's not what I meant." He accepted her chastise with a shrug and then spoke directly to her son. "Your mommy's right—before you do things like snowboarding and horse riding, you need lots of lessons."

"One day," she said, and looked a little relieved he'd made an attempt to defuse her son's enthusiasm. "I promise."

The pancakes arrived, and Jake watched as T.J. devoured the food within minutes. The kid certainly had a healthy appetite. Abby was still stirring her tea. Jake observed her out of the corner of his eye. Even on edge—which she clearly was—Abby was still incredibly pretty. He *still* thought she was the most beautiful woman he had ever known. Which made him an idiot. But it was hard to shake off the past. Hard to stop remembering everything they had been to one another. They'd been an item for the last year of high school. Their relationship had been passionate and yet, at times, surprisingly companionable. Back then, he'd been head over heels in love with her. Loving Abby had made hating his father bearable. She made his life better, and naturally Jake had believed their relationship would go the distance. Even if that distance was him joining the army and ending up in a war zone while Abby remained in Cedar River.

But Abby had bailed once he'd made his intentions clear. She didn't want to be a soldier's wife. Of course, he knew why. Her mother had been one. Her mother had lost her husband and had had very little time for Abby once the grief set in. And it didn't matter how many times Jake assured her that he had every intention of surviving deployment—Abby wasn't swayed. Because, of course, he couldn't give her guarantees. Rationally, he knew that. As she did. But back then, being so young and determined, he'd imagined they could work through their differences. But he was wrong. She'd given him an ultimatum—the military or their relationship. Jake left for boot camp two months after graduation. Abby married someone else, and he didn't speak to her again until Tom's funeral.

That was ages ago now, and best forgotten. There was little point in thinking about the past. The future was what mattered. And Jake's future was back in Sacramento. With his work and his friends and the life he'd made for himself. Not Cedar River.

And not Abby Perkins—despite how much the memory of her haunted his dreams.

"I gotta go," he said and swiftly got to his feet. "It was nice to meet you, T.J.," he said and looked at Abby. "Take care, Abby."

Then he left as though his heels were on fire.

"Mommy?"

Abby tucked the blanket in around her son and sat on the edge of his bed. "Yes, T.J."

"How are babies made?"

She looked at her son. "Remember that book we read together a while ago," she reminded him.

He nodded, regarding her thoughtfully. "About how the daddy and mommy make the baby and it grows in the mommy's belly?"

"That's right."

"Is that how you made me?" he asked, his small hand touching her stomach.

"Exactly," she replied. "I made you with your daddy, and you grew inside me and then you were born."

His innocent gaze narrowed. "How come I don't look like my daddy?"

She sucked in a sharp breath and chose her next words carefully. "I'll tell you something. You look exactly like your dad."

He smiled quizzically. "I do?"

She touched her face. "In every way that counts."

He accepted her explanation with a grin. "Can you tell me the story about my angel daddy?"

Tom.

Tell him the truth. Now.

My god, what a mess I've made of things...

Guilt pressed down hard on her shoulders. She thought

about the picture of her husband on the mantel in the living room, taken on their wedding day. Tom was smiling, his auburn hair shining beneath the afternoon sun. It had been a happy day. Back then, things had seemed so simple. Marriage, children, her work…everyday things that made up a full life. Except that there were no children and she knew how devastated Tom was when they discovered he would be unable to make her pregnant. They discussed using a sperm donor, even made a few plans to go down that road, but she suspected her husband wasn't completely signed on to the idea. He wanted his own children, and sadly, he would never know the joy.

"Well, he really wanted to have a little boy just like you. It was all he talked about. But he got sick. And you were born after he died, and since then he's been your angel daddy and watches over you."

T.J. bit his bottom lip. "I wish I still had a daddy."

Abby's insides lurched. "I know you do. One day, very soon," she said and hugged him close, "I promise you'll have a real daddy."

He brows shot up. "I will?"

She nodded. "Yes."

"Like my friends Tim and Benson have daddies?" he asked, eyes wide.

She inhaled deeply. "Exactly like that."

"Yay, Mommy," he said and then his eyes widened even farther. "I can't wait," he said and then looked worried. "But what if he doesn't like me?"

"Of course he'll like you," she promised and felt her heart tightening in her chest. "You're adorable and the best little boy in the whole world."

He giggled. "You have to say that, 'cause you're my mommy."

She smiled. "I love you more than anything."

"I love you, too, Mommy."

"Good night, sweetie," she said and kissed her son good-night.

Once T.J. was settled, she took a shower, dressed in her pajamas and spent an hour in the kitchen, lingering over a pot of green tea, thinking about how T.J. was asking more questions every day, and about how she was going to tell Jake he had a son. She didn't doubt he'd be furious with her for keeping the truth from him.

She was on the dinner shift at the hotel for the next few days—perhaps she'd run into him and find a chance to start a conversation. Maybe he'd be open to talking… maybe he'd say it was okay. Perhaps she was imagining the worst for no reason. Jake was a reasonable man. Surely he'd see the logic in her decision to conceal the truth about T.J.'s paternity for as long as she had.

By the time she arrived at the hotel the following afternoon, Abby had almost convinced herself that the transition from Jake not knowing he had a son to discovering the truth about T.J. would be seamless.

She did the shift change with the lunch chef, discussing a few last-minute alterations to the evening menu, and then talked the new sous chef through the prep work they needed to do. The restaurant was booked solid for the next few days, although tonight was unusually quiet, and she made a mental note to ask Connie Rickard, the hotel's assistant manager, about the possibilty of taking some much-needed time off for the following week. Connie was married to Liam's half brother and she'd always considered the other woman a friend. Connie would understand if Abby said she needed some personal time. By five, the kitchen was prepped and ready to go and Abby took a short break, hanging out by the piano near the bar, sipping on a soda and lime.

"Everything okay, Abby?"

It was Liam O'Sullivan, her boss. She swiveled on the stool and nodded. "Sure. Just taking ten before the dinner rush starts."

He smiled. Abby had always liked Liam. He was a good employer—fair and very approachable. And he'd done wonders for the hotel since taking over from his father. The O'Sullivans were rich and the most prominent family in town, a little entitled and sometimes too big for their boots, but they had a strong sense of charity and goodwill, particularly Liam.

"I have a business meeting in my office this evening—any chance you could rustle up a few snacks for around eight o'clock?" he asked.

"Of course."

"I'd like you to hang around for a while, if that's okay. Some of what's being discussed will affect you."

"Me?"

He waved a hand. "The restaurant. The kitchen. Nothing sinister, so you can stop looking concerned. Just a few improvements to the way the place runs. Connie will be there, too."

Abby spent the next few hours running the kitchen, preparing meals and thinking about how she was going to tell Jake he had a son.

At a few minutes to eight, Abby left the kitchen in the competent hands of the sous chef and headed upstairs to Liam's office suite. She had her own swipe card to access the elevator to the floor and was quickly in the reception area, carrying a tray of food. Connie came out to greet her and she chatted to her friend for a moment. If she wasn't mistaken, Abby believed she spotted a tiny baby bump concealed beneath the other woman's corporate jacket. Her husband worked for an architectural firm in Rapid

City. But since Abby wasn't one to pry, she didn't ask or speculate any further.

They walked into Liam's office, and Abby stopped in her tracks.

Jake was sitting on the leather chesterfield, an electronic tablet in his hand. He looked up when she entered the room, offered a modest half smile and then dropped his gaze.

"You guys know one another, right?" Liam said and moved around his desk.

She nodded. "Yes."

"Abby and I go way back."

She glanced at him and felt heat rise up her neck.

"I've been talking to Jake about installing a new security system in the hotel—including the kitchen in the restaurant and the bistro, and the rear parking area behind the employee entrance," Liam explained and offered her a seat on the chesterfield. "I just wanted your thoughts on the idea."

She sat down, conscious that Jake was barely a foot away from her. She crossed her ankles, noticing there was sauce splattered on the front of her apron, and she realized she was still wearing her chef's hat. And probably looked as though she'd been in a hot kitchen for the last few hours.

I don't care if Jake thinks I look like a washed-out rag.

She worked—she was a single mom. She had every right to look tired and washed out.

Abby listened as Liam, Connie and Jake discussed the proposal for a more efficient and safer security system for the hotel, and she offered a couple of comments when they broached the subject of the restaurant and maintaining staff and patron privacy while monitoring who came and went during the course of the day.

"The hotel and the restaurants are getting busier every year," Liam said. "And with more business comes the potential for more risk. I want to minimize that risk…can you do that?"

Jake nodded. "Absolutely. My company has worked with several hotels in Sacramento and San Francisco and one in Vegas. I'll spend the next few days looking over the place and come back to you at the end of the week with some suggestions."

Connie moved forward and passed him a swipe card. "You'll need this to move freely around the hotel."

"And touch base with Abby if you need any information about the restaurant or bistro," Liam said and nodded. "She's worked as the manager in the bistro and the main restaurant as well as head chef…she knows the running of that part of the business better than anyone."

As much as she was flattered by Liam's words, the idea of working closely with Jake on a business proposal for the hotel turned Abby's stomach. It was bad enough she had to face him with news about T.J.'s paternity…anything else was out of the question.

Abby got up and excused herself. Once she was back downstairs in the safe haven of her kitchen, she relaxed a fraction and took a couple of long breaths. The sous chef reported that nothing was amiss, all meals had been served and there was only one table of patrons still lingering over their wine. Relieved that she wouldn't have to hang around until midnight, as sometimes happened, Abby chatted to the duty manager about the following evening's menu and then ensured the kitchen was prepped and ready for the following morning. Once she was done she headed for the locker room and ditched her hat and apron, changed her shoes and dumped her black sneakers into her tote and headed back through the kitchen and into the restaurant, immediately spotting Jake standing by the bar.

"Got a minute?" he asked.

She sighed. "Sure," she said and walked behind the bar. "What would you like?"

"Club soda," he replied.

"You don't drink?" she asked as she poured soda into two glasses and added a wedge of lime.

"Not really."

"Because of your dad?"

"Because I don't see the point in getting wasted," he replied and then nodded. "And yeah, because of Billie-Jack. You know how he was."

"I remember."

"I didn't want to end up like him."

"You're nothing like him," she said firmly and pushed the glasses across the bar.

"Thanks," he said, and she wondered if he was thanking her for the drink, or her words.

"How did you get involved in this project?" she asked as she moved around the bar and sat on a stool beside him.

He shrugged. "I was talking to Kieran the other day. I figured he must have told his brother what I do. Your boss approached me this morning. And here I am."

Abby looked at him, taking in the dark trousers, white shirt, polished shoes. He looked like a businessman. And utterly gorgeous. "I don't image you wear that getup on your bike?"

He grinned. "No. I'm definitely more comfortable in jeans and a T-shirt…but sometimes the business means I have to dress the part. And you know how your boss is known for being an uptight workaholic."

"I didn't realize the Culhanes and the O'Sullivans were on such friendly terms."

"We're not," he replied. "It's business."

"Liam's not so uptight these days," she said and grabbed her tote. "He got married and had a baby a couple of years ago. Kids have a way of putting what's important into perspective."

His brow came up. "Is that what it did for you?"

Abby nodded, feeling heat rise through her blood.

Do it! Tell him!

"T.J. is the most important thing in my life."

"Of course. He seems like a good kid."

"He is," she said and inhaled. "He's smart, sometimes too smart for his own good, and he can be willful, but he—"

"He gets that from you," Jake said and grinned devilishly. "I mean, Tom was pretty easygoing and agreeable. But you're nothing like that."

"He's very much like his father," Abby said and swallowed hard, realizing she had a real window, an opportunity to tell the truth. Good conscience made her grab for it, even though she was trembling inside and they were at her workplace and the setting was wildly inappropriate to receive such news. But a window was a window. And since her gumption was in short supply, she needed to take opportunity when it arose. "In fact, he's like—"

"Hey, Abby?"

The sous chef poked his head around the kitchen doorway, and the words she was so close to saying collapsed on the edge of her tongue. "Yes…what?"

"We've got a vegan party of six coming in tomorrow night," he said and shrugged. "Just giving you a heads-up. It'll be a big off-the-menu order."

She nodded. "Okay, thank you."

The chef quickly disappeared, and she noticed that Jake was smiling broadly. "Troublesome vegans?"

She offered a tight smile. "They're regulars. They like this vegetable stack I make…which isn't on the menu, and probably should be, but since we're in beef country, Liam has this thing about keeping it real for the locals. Even though his wife, Kayla, is a vegetarian and—"

"Abby," he said and drank some soda. "Calm down. You've no reason to be nervous around me."

If only he knew…

She shrugged, galvanized by the need to do what was right, but knowing that an unexpected announcement about her son's paternity at the bar wasn't appropriate. "I was wondering… I was thinking about getting T.J. a snowboard for Christmas and remembered how you said you'd teach him to snowboard. I thought maybe lessons would benefit him beforehand, you know, so that he gets some practice. Only if you meant it, of course. I mean, you'll probably be leaving town soon and I—"

"I told you I was staying for a while. And I always mean what I say," he remarked.

Of course he did. Typical Jake. He'd never been one to shy from the truth in any situation. "So…yes?"

He looked at her for a moment—almost warily, and then slowly nodded. "Sure. There've been a few good snowfalls on Peaks Ridge. I'll let you know when the weather is right, and we'll make a date."

A date with Jake…

Her insides crunched up, and she nodded. "Great. Thank you."

Of course, it wasn't a real date. She wasn't interested in going down that road. It was about connecting T.J. with his father, about building relationships, about undoing the wrong she committed six years earlier.

"Are you okay, Abby?"

She managed a tight smile. "Would you like to come over for dinner Friday night? Maybe hang out with T.J.

for a while…you know, to see how he feels about snow-boarding lessons. It's my next night off, so I can cook."

He looked at her oddly for a second, as though he couldn't quite believe her invitation. Then he shrugged. "Ah…okay."

"I'll make brownies," she added, remembering that years earlier they had been his favorite dessert, and clutched her tote. "So, see you Friday, around six o'clock."

He nodded and slid off the bar stool. "I'll stop by here tomorrow if that's okay…to go over the security proposal for O'Sullivan, to look at the kitchen and staffing area, that kind of thing. I'll touch base with the restaurant manager, and we can go through a few things together. What time does your shift start?"

"Three," she replied. "I can meet you at two thirty, if that's convenient?"

"It is," he said. "See you tomorrow."

"'Bye, Jake," she said and watched as he turned and left the restaurant.

She sighed and stared at the empty doorway. *Small steps*, she told herself.

But she had to tell Jake that he was T.J.'s father…and soon.

Chapter Five

"Are you sure you couldn't find a bigger tree?"

Jake was at the ranch late on Thursday afternoon, drinking coffee with Mitch, Hank, Joss and their cousin David, and looking at the biggest indoor Christmas tree he'd ever seen. The thing was so tall it reached the ceiling. And it was decorated within an inch of its life.

Mitch hitched a thumb in David's direction. "Blame him. He's the one who has the trees on his ranch."

Jake grinned. "You selling trees now?"

David laughed. "Only to family and friends. There's still half a dozen left if anyone wants one. Nothing that big, though."

"I use a fake tree," Joss remarked and made a face.

"Philistine," Mitch said and then shrugged and grinned. "I know it's ridiculously large, but it's what my soon-to-be wife wanted."

The wedding was planned for a couple of weeks before Christmas, and Jake knew Mitch was over the moon about the prospect.

"Happy wife, happy life?" Hank said and chuckled.

"Something like that," their elder brother replied. "But I'm not complaining. I love seeing her happy, and I love having Tess back at the ranch. It's like things are back to how they should be. Besides, you know I always liked being married." He paused and watched them. "You guys should try it sometime."

Hank laughed nervously and tugged at his collar. "Ah, time for me to get back to work."

"You can all joke if you like," Mitch said seriously. "But I mean it. Family is everything. And we're stronger together, as a family."

"Lightning doesn't strike twice," Joss said, a hint of bitterness in his tone. "Anyway, I'm not sure any woman could put up with me the way Lara did. And I need to put the girls first. *If* I got married again, she would be taking on another woman's children—that's a big deal and not something I'd do lightly."

"Agreed," Mitch said and nodded and then looked at Jake. "What about you?"

Jake met Mitch's stare and shrugged. "We don't all get a perfect happily-ever-after, and I'm not willing to—"

"Put yourself out there?" Mitch suggested and raised a brow.

"Settle," Jake supplied and shrugged. "But if you must know, I actually have a date tomorrow night. At least, I *think* it's a date."

"With who?" Joss asked the obvious question.

"Abby," he replied and shrugged again. He saw that his three brothers were staring at him incredulously. "Don't look so shocked. I volunteered to teach her kid to snowboard. Then she invited me over for dinner."

Mitch made a surprised face. "And how do you feel about that?"

His mouth twitched. "I don't really know. Abby and I have history, and not all of it is good. She married my best friend, remember?"

"Because you left town," Joss reminded him.

"I know," he remarked and then took a long breath. "I guess, back then, I thought she'd wait. Stupid, huh?"

"You mean being young and in love and hopeful?"

Mitch remarked and shrugged lightly. "Not really. I think back then we all believed you and Abby would end up together."

"You guys were the perfect couple in high school," Joss said and grinned. "The good girl and the bad boy… it was like a romance movie in the making."

Memory swirled around in his head, and he grimaced at his brother's amused words. But the truth was, back then he *had* believed he and Abby would go the distance. He knew she didn't want to be a soldier's wife, but he'd been sure their relationship was strong enough to get past her grief from losing her dad at such a young age. Killed by friendly fire in Desert Storm, Colin Reed had died when Abby was three years old and her mom never recovered from the loss of her beloved husband. Despite Jake assuring her how *unlikely* it would be that he would be injured, or worse, she wasn't swayed. So they broke up. And months later she was dating his best friend.

"Nothing's that perfect," he said quietly.

"Oh, I don't know," Joss mused. "Lara and I never had a serious misunderstanding the whole time we were together."

"That's because Lara was a saint," Hank said and laughed. "She had to be to put up with you. You'd need a saint, too," he said and looked at Jake.

Jake smiled to himself, uneasy *and* slightly amused at the idea he was the object of his brother's teasing banter. His siblings were a tight unit, and he'd often felt excluded from their good-natured rivalry and dissing. His own fault, of course, since he'd stayed away for so long. But now he was back, albeit temporarily, he liked the idea of getting to know them all better and being a part of their lives.

"So, is this like a romantic date? The kind that you bring flowers to?" Joss asked and grinned.

"No," Jake replied. "I'm pretty sure it's just about her kid."

Joss nodded and looked at him intensely for a moment. "I think he's in Sissy's advanced math class."

Joss's eldest daughter was eleven. Jake frowned. "Is he a math prodigy?"

His brother shrugged. "Don't know. Just a smart kid, from all accounts. But a handful, I believe."

Jake could believe it. "Well, Tom was a smart guy."

Mitch made a face. "Didn't you used to do his math homework?"

Funny, he'd forgotten that. "Sometimes. He used to miss classes because of his allergies. And you remember how his parents were? Nice people, but they had high expectations."

"At least they cared," Hank said and laughed humorlessly, and suddenly they were all remembering Billie-Jack and his bad parenting.

"Anyone know where he is?" Joss asked.

Jake shook his head. "Don't know, don't care."

"I think Grant knows," Mitch said of their youngest brother.

"As long as he's not in Cedar River," Hank said, harsher than usual.

Mitch raised his coffee mug. "Here's to being a better human being than the old man."

They all followed suit, and once the coffee was finished, Jake got to his feet. "Well, I'm outta here. See you this weekend."

"You sure you don't want to crash here tonight?" Mitch asked.

"No, but thanks," he replied. "I have a meeting with

O'Sullivan in the morning and need to crunch a few numbers."

"Fraternizing with the enemy, huh?" Joss said and laughed.

"I thought we were all past the schoolyard rivalry with the O'Sullivans?" he remarked and grabbed his keys.

"We are," Hank said and elbowed his twin in the ribs. "He's just sour because the O'Sullivans raised the rent on the garage."

Joss scowled. "They own sixty percent of all the commercial property in town and hike the rents up when the mood strikes."

"That's commerce," Jake said and grinned.

"That's robbery. But since you've joined the millionaire's club yourself," Joss said and grinned back, "you've gone all corporate and white collar."

"Millionaire's club?" Jake shot back. "That's a gross exaggeration."

He didn't tell his brothers the buy-out offer he and his business partner had recently received would certainly put him in that category. They were still mulling over the proposition. Trent had family in Sacramento, so he would certainly stay on there, but since Jake's family was in Cedar River, there was nothing tying him to California should they decide to accept the offer.

Which meant what? Move back? Start afresh? He wasn't sure he'd know how.

He left the ranch a few minutes later and headed into town, stopping by the cemetery on his way through. Tom's grave was easy to find, and he noticed fresh flowers had been placed in front of the headstone, which said, Tomas John Perkins. Son. Brother. Husband. Friend.

Looking at his friend's resting place, Jake experienced an acute feeling of sadness and regret. He glanced at the flowers and figured they'd been placed there by Abby and her son. Jake was glad Tom was remembered so fondly. Abby had clearly loved him, and still did, by all accounts. And why not—Tom had been a good man. One of the best. And he understood why Abby had been drawn to the other man. Tom had offered her everything Jake didn't—security, stability, the reality of knowing people were safe from harm in her world. Of course, no one was truly safe. Tom had died, and she was alone.

Except for her son and her grandmother.

Jake sighed, turned, headed back to his bike. The weather had turned bleak in the past hour, and a heavy cloud hung overhead. He grabbed his helmet, sat on the bike and drove back into town. By the time he pulled up into the hotel parking area, a soft blanket of snow had fallen. He strode through the foyer and spotted Liam O'Sullivan by the concierge desk. The follow-up meeting they'd had the day before had gone well, and he was sure they'd get the job. Not that he really needed the work, but he liked the idea of doing something in his hometown. And catching up with Abby and the restaurant manager a couple of days earlier had been relatively tension-free.

The restaurant manager was a woman in her midtwenties and was happy to answer any questions. She spoke openly about Abby in glowing terms and Jake admired the way Abby was so well respected at the hotel. The other woman made it very clear how much she appreciated Abby's input and expertise when it came to the day-to-day running of the hotel restaurant. Once the meeting was over and they were alone, Abby reconfirmed their date, although not exactly calling it a date—but since he was going to her house and meeting her kid again, he figured it was *sort* of a date.

Jake wasn't sure how he felt about it. Sure, he wanted to mend fences, but seeing Abby socially wasn't something he'd planned on doing when he came back to Cedar River. There was their complicated past to consider. And his lingering attraction to think about. Denying he was still attracted to Abby was pointless. She was the first girl he'd loved. In fact, she was the *only* girl he'd loved. It might be in the past, but the memories were acute.

Whatever had happened in the past, Jake was determined to make sure he left Cedar River with a clear conscience. And his heart intact.

"Mommy?"

Abby glanced toward her son, who was sitting at the kitchen table, drawing and clearly creating a masterpiece with his crayons. "Yes, honey."

"Can we get our Christmas tree tomorrow?"

She sighed. T.J. had been complaining about their lack of a tree all week. "We'll try, okay. I have to borrow a truck and—"

"But how will Santa know where to put the presents if there's no tree?"

Her son's relentless logic always made her think. "Don't worry, by the time Christmas Eve comes around, we'll have a tree."

He regarded her thoughtfully, seemed happy with her reply and then nodded. "What time is Gran coming over?"

"She's not," Abby replied and smiled. "Remember how I said she was going to her friend Maree's place to play mah-jongg? But I did invite someone for dinner."

His eyes widened. "Who?"

"You remember my friend Jake."

T.J.'s mouth twisted thoughtfully. "The man who bought our breakfast?"

She nodded. "That's right. He'll be here soon."

Which is why my hands are shaking...

"Yay," T.J. said and grinned. "I really liked him, Mommy."

Abby sucked in a breath and kept tossing the salad she'd prepared to accompany the lasagna in the oven. It was her son's favorite and their usual fare on the Friday evenings when she didn't have to work. Rostered off for the next three days, Abby figured that gave her ample time to talk to Jake and tell him about T.J.

If he turned up.

He hadn't looked overly thrilled by her suggestion they have dinner. Or her agreement for him to give T.J. snowboarding lessons. Okay, so maybe she *had* done an abrupt turnaround and surprised him with her request. After all, she hadn't really given him any indication that she wanted to spend time with him. A week ago she'd made it clear that they didn't need to be friends and their past was exactly that.

Abby heard an unfamiliar roar coming from outside and realized the sound was a motorcycle. She quickly pulled off her apron, wiped her hands and headed from the room. She checked her appearance in the hallway mirror and stopped midstride. *Pale*. And anxious. Not surprising, she figured. But she didn't want Jake thinking there was something wrong. She wanted the evening to go smoothly…like a casual meet and greet. She wanted T.J. to get to know Jake and to observe how they connected *before* she told Jake the truth.

She pinched her cheeks, foolishly wishing for a moment that she'd spent the time to add a little makeup to her face and maybe do her hair into something other than her standard weekend ponytail. Too late now, she mused as she heard the motorbike engine shut down. T.J. came racing down the hallway, and she gently steered him to stay behind her. And then she opened the door.

Jake was striding up the path, his shoulders covered in a light blanket of snow. The weather had changed over the last few days, and she suspected they were in for a long, cold winter. He wore jeans, boots, a leather jacket and gloves and held his helmet in his hands.

"Evening," he said when he reached the door and shook the snow from his hair. "Snow. Who would have thought."

Abby watched the motion, remembering how much she'd once loved running her fingertips through his hair. Back in high school it had been longer, and not the military crew cut he now wore. Back in high school, so many things had been different. For one, Jake hadn't left her heartbroken. And two, she hadn't sought comfort in the arms and heart of his best friend.

"A bit of a change from Sacramento, I imagine?" she asked.

"Just a bit," he replied.

"Do you remember me?"

T.J.'s voice rang out between them.

"I certainly do," Jake replied and smiled, and her heart flipped over when she realized her son had the exact same dimple in his cheek. They were so alike she was certain an onlooker would be able to make the connection if they were seen together. Which meant telling Jake the truth as soon as possible was now imperative. "How you doing, buddy?"

"I'm good, thanks," T.J. replied. "I got a new book this week, one with dragons and sword fights and everything."

"Sounds like a great read," Jake said easily.

"You can borrow it if you want."

"Please, come inside," she said before Jake could respond, opening the door wider, gesturing to a side table and coatrack in the hallway. "You can leave your jacket and helmet there."

He nodded, ditched his gloves and helmet and placed his jacket on a hook. "Nice house."

Abby managed a tight smile. "I like it. And it's next door to Gran, so that's a bonus."

His brows came up. "Is your grandmother here tonight?"

She shook her head. "No. Just us," she said and realized how intimate it sounded.

He didn't react. But lord, he was so gorgeous she could barely draw a breath. Her heart was skipping wildly, and she was certain her skin was flushed. She took a couple of steps, and he followed until they were in living room doorway. "Ah...the kitchen...we should..."

"Where's your tree?" he asked, noticing the conspicuous space by the window. "You love Christmas...at least you used to."

"I still do," she said quickly. "I just haven't had time to go and pick up a tree. Or a car big enough. And I don't have racks on the roof of my Honda."

Beside her, T.J. groaned. "See, Mommy...everyone knows that we should have a tree by now."

Abby sighed. "Okay...we'll get a tree tomorrow."

"What if they have sold out?" her son asked, looking seriously mortified by the idea.

"They won't," Jake quickly assured him, and Abby sent him an appreciative glance. "In fact, I know someone who has plenty of trees left. We could go and get one tomorrow?" he suggested, looking directly at Abby.

"Ah...from who?"

"My cousin David," he explained. "He has trees growing on his ranch, so he's got a small sales lot that he opened this season. Tess and Mitch have one the size of a house in their living room. So, yes?"

"Please, Mommy," T.J. said excitedly. "Say yes! Say yes!"

Abby found herself nodding. "Okay…that sounds good."

T.J. raced down the hallway and beckoned them to follow him.

"He's a great kid," Jake remarked as her son disappeared around the corner.

She smiled nervously. "You've made his day. His week," she added and sighed. "He's been at me all week to get a tree. But with work and everything else, I haven't had the time to—"

"I'll pick you up in the morning, around nine," Jake said quietly. "If that works for you."

She nodded. "Sure."

The mood between them was oddly intimate and Abby's skin turned hot all over, despite the weather outside. He was close, and so tall and broad shouldered, and the cologne he wore was a woodsy scent that assailed her foolish senses. It had been such a long time since they'd been alone together—not in a restaurant or café—but in her home. And not that they were truly alone, because her son was in the next room. *Their son.* And suddenly the reality *and* enormity of the situation hit her with the force of a freight train.

"Abby? What's wrong?"

His voice, so deep, so familiar, wound up her spine. "I… Jake…we… I have to—"

"Mommy?"

T.J.'s happy voice cut through her stammering, and she sucked in a long breath. Jake was watching her, staring down because he was almost a foot taller than she was, and then he touched her face. It was almost involuntary. As though he was willed to move despite himself. Because she saw uncertainty and conflict in his expression. His thumb stroked her cheek for a brief second and then he dropped his hand, still watching her with blistering intensity.

She turned and spotted T.J. standing by the doorway, looking eager and happy. Male company. Of course. Her son rarely had the opportunity to spend time with a man. Other than one teacher at his school and his soccer coach, he was surrounded by women. And right now, he was standing in the same space as his father…a stranger…and yet he looked delighted and excited by the idea that a real live man was in their house. She remembered how he'd talked about having a father—one that was real and not just a picture on the mantel. And then guilt—by the bucket load—pressed down her shoulders and she could barely stand.

"Are you okay?"

Jake again. Concerned and clearly seeing her reaction.

"I'm fine," she lied. "Just tired."

His gaze narrowed. "If you want me to bail, I can—"

"No," she said quickly and waved a hand. "I'll be okay. And I cooked, so it would be a tragedy for you to miss out on my famous lasagna."

He grinned, and his eyes had never seemed greener. He held a up a small brown bag. "I brought cider. But I can duck out and get wine if you'd prefer."

She shook her head. "I'm not much of a drinker, remember?"

"Me, either, remember?"

She remembered everything. Billie-Jack's penchant for drunkenness had cemented something inside him about overindulgence. When they were young, it had seemed at odds with his bad-boy persona. Not that he was *all* bad. With her, Jake had always been considerate and gentle and undeniably protective.

By the time they reached the kitchen, her nerves had

settled a little, but she was acutely conscious of Jake behind her. He remained on the other side of the counter as she moved around to the sink, and T.J. quickly propped himself up on a stool beside the man who clearly fascinated him.

"Jake?" Her son's voice cut through the sudden silence. "Can I ride your motorbike?"

"No," he replied quietly and glanced in her direction. "Not until you're twenty-one."

T.J.'s eyes rolled dramatically. "But that's *forever.*"

Jake grinned. "When's your birthday?"

"March third," her son announced loudly.

Abby waited, watching as Jake took a few moments, wondering if he was working out the math calculation in his head from the day they'd slept together and knowing he come up almost two months short. He didn't know T.J. was premature. No one in Cedar River did other than her grandmother. When he replied, there was no query in his words. "Not forever. Just five thousand, one hundred and ninety-four days."

T.J.'s eyes widened disbelievingly. "You can do math really fast, like me!"

Abby's whole body clenched. Of course, her son would find common ground with Jake, but the idea it was happening so fast filled her with dread. She didn't have much time. Jake was a smart guy. Too smart. If she didn't come clean soon, he'd work it out for himself.

She grabbed glasses for the cider and discreetly observed her son and Jake interacting. *Their son.* The salad was done, and she took cutlery and plates to the table, aware that Jake was watching her movements. Something uncurled inside her. And she knew, without a doubt, that nothing had changed.

It's still there...

The awareness. The attraction. The connection that drew them together from the very beginning. It was easy to remember what loving Jake had felt like. Easier still to recall his touch, the taste of his kiss, his breath against her skin. Making love with Jake had always been more than simple sex. Even that last time, when they were both grieving, both reeling from the loss of someone they'd both loved, there had been an intensity about the moment that still had the power to reach her to the core. And now, years later, he was in her kitchen, and they were acting absurdly normal, and he had no idea the child who was now looking at him with budding hero worship was the child he'd gifted her that afternoon so many years ago.

She instructed T.J. to take a seat at the table, and Jake quickly moved around the counter. The kitchen immediately seemed smaller with him in it, and she felt his nearness like a cloak enveloping her.

"Need some help?" he asked.

She nodded and passed him the salad bowl and bread basket. "Thank you."

"My pleasure."

She tried to ignore the sexy way his eyes glittered. And failed. "Um…are you still prepared to teach T.J. how to ride a snowboard?"

"Of course."

"Great. I wasn't going to purchase gear until I was sure he was interested in doing it, but obviously he'll need a board. I think Gran has a couple of old boards in her garage."

He frowned and then grinned. "If you mean those same old boards that we used when we were kids, the ones that you picked up at that yard sale, forget it. Remember when you crashed yours and split it down the center?"

Abby did remember. She'd taken a tumble and hit her

head. Jake had been at her side in a microsecond and then carried her back down the mountain. And he'd sworn not to take her again without the proper safety equipment.

"I still have a scar here," she said and touched her temple.

His gaze was rivetingly intense. "I don't think I've ever been as scared in my life as I was in the fifteen seconds it took me to get from where I was to where you'd crashed into that tree."

It was quite the revelation. And couldn't possibly be true. He'd been a war zone. He'd been a witness to the car wreck that had almost killed his brother Hank. He'd returned to Cedar River to be by Mitch's hospital bed when the other man had suffered life-threatening injuries. Much more intense situations than her tumble in the snow. But Jake didn't lie. For all his faults, he was always honest about who he was. He'd never lied to her about joining the military, never made her believe he would change his mind.

"I didn't realize…"

He didn't respond for a moment. Didn't do anything other than look directly at her. "I'll borrow some gear from Joss," he said quietly. "I know he takes his girls snowboarding and has plenty of safety gear."

She nodded in agreement and grabbed the lasagna. Dinner was quickly on the table, and sitting opposite him, it occurred to Abby that this was the first time she'd had a man at her dinner table since Tom. She didn't date, didn't entertain, didn't really have any male friends she could call upon for companionship or anything else. She'd only ever had two lovers—her husband and Jake. Not exactly a prude, but since she and Jake had gotten together in senior year and she'd begun dating Tom just months after they broke up, she'd never had the time or opportunity to consider being with anyone else. And she wasn't wired the casual sex kind of way. Sure, she liked sex as much as the next person, and had missed having it in her life the last few years, but she was a mother first and foremost, and she wasn't in a position to enter into a casual sexual relationship with anyone.

Even Jake.

Where did that come from?

Sure, the attraction was still there…she was savvy enough to register the awareness building between them. But she had more important things to concentrate on… like telling Jake he had a son.

"So, T.J.," she said as she broke a piece of bread into pieces. "Jake has agreed to teach you how to snowboard."

Her son's eyes grew as wide as saucers. "Yay!"

"But there are rules," she added. "You have to listen to everything he says. And no tantrums if you fall off, okay?"

Her son was a perfectionist by nature, and she knew he struggled with understanding why some activities were beyond his physical capabilities because of his age. But she wasn't worried about him being safe. She knew Jake would take care of him, knew he could be trusted to ensure her son followed the rules.

"I promise, Mommy," T.J. said and grinned happily.

"How about Sunday?" Jake suggested.

"Yay," her son said again, clearly delighted by the prospect.

"You can supervise," Jake said quietly, looking at her. "Or join in."

"Yes, Mommy," T.J. said excitedly. "We can all go snowboarding."

She smiled toward her son. "I'll think about it."

T.J. grinned, then put down his fork, chewing the food that was in his mouth before he asked a question she was completely unprepared for.

"Mommy, is Jake your new boyfriend?"

Chapter Six

Jake wasn't sure who was made more uncomfortable by the child's unexpected question. He fought the sudden impulse to tug on his collar. Instead, he watched as color rose up Abby's neck and smacked her cheeks. Still, she looked cute when she was embarrassed. Beautiful, in fact. And in her jeans and red sweater, with her hair up and her face free of makeup, he couldn't remember ever seeing her look more attractive.

"Ah...well..." she said, her voice trailing off. "No, and I don't think that's—"

"Kenny Diaz's mommy has a boyfriend," T.J. said matter-of-factly. "But he lives with them all of the time. Kenny's daddy is in heaven, like my angel daddy."

Jake saw something undeniably raw in Abby's expression. *Angel daddy.* Tom, of course. It was a nice way to honor the memory of the child's father. "I knew your dad," Jake said gently. "He was my best friend in school."

The boy's eyes widened. "He's my angel daddy," he corrected. "Because he died and watches over me, but Mommy says one day I'll —"

"T.J.," Abby said quietly. "Why don't you finish your dinner. It's your favorite."

He nodded. "Sure, Mommy. And then can I read my new book?"

"Of course."

Jake listened to their exchange and smiled to himself.

He felt sad for his friend, thinking how Tom would never get to experience a conversation with the boy, or sit at the dinner table with him, or teach him how to snowboard. The truth was, Jake liked the idea of spending time with his friend's son more than he'd imagined he would. For the last decade, and particularly since he'd left the military, he'd avoided doing anything that resembled *anything* like domesticity. He'd dated several women in the last couple of years, but never longer than a few months, ending things before he could get too settled or in too deep. And he had never dated anyone with children. The truth was, he'd had little to do with kids. Sure, he imagined he'd get married and have his own children one day, but that meant commitment. And, of course, falling in love. Being in a relationship with someone who already had kids—or a *kid*—was something else altogether.

Not that he was thinking about that in relation to Abby. It was simply dinner, for heaven's sake. And the promise to teach her son to snowboard. Besides, they had way too much history, and he was leaving soon. Maybe not immediately…but soon. Which meant starting something in Cedar River was out of the question. Even if, at times, it did feel as though they had unfinished business. But it wasn't anything he was prepared to pursue or contemplate.

Once dinner was eaten and the dishes were cleared, her son left the room.

"He's a great kid, Abby," he remarked and drank some cider. "You should be really proud of him."

"I am," she replied and moved around the kitchen counter.

Jake got to his feet and stood on the other side of the countertop. "Tom would be, too. It's nice you named him after his father."

Her eyes shone brightly. "I felt it was the right thing to do."

He nodded and then asked a question that had been nagging at his brain for the last week. "Why didn't Tom's parents stay in town? I lost touch with them years ago." The truth was, Jake hadn't had anything to do with Tom's folks since Tom and Abby had hooked up. But he always remembered them fondly. "I find it strange they left when they had a—"

"Memories," she said, cutting him. "Sometimes they make a person stay. Sometimes they make a person leave."

He knew exactly what she meant. Jake had left Cedar River to join the military and exorcise the rage and resentment he felt toward his father, and to help make him a better man. One who was controlled and disciplined and fully in charge of himself. And for the most part, Jake believed he'd succeeded. He always endeavored to be the most authentic version of himself.

"You know, Abby, when high school was over, I never really believed you'd end things between us," he admitted. "I thought you'd...wait. Back then I was so determined to be the exact opposite of Billie-Jack, I don't think I really considered the consequences."

She stopped the task she was doing and turned to face him. "I watched my mother grieve a husband she lost to war...and like you, I didn't want to end up as a shadow of my parent."

"So, it was gridlock?"

She nodded. "Exactly. We both wanted different things back then. And I don't regret marrying Tom for one moment."

"You shouldn't," he said and shrugged. "Tom was a good man. The best."

"Strange," she said and sighed. "That's what he used to say about you."

Jake could believe it. He and Tom had been firm friends. To some, theirs appeared an unusual alliance, he figured. Tom Perkins came from a traditional middle-class family. He had an older sister, Trudy, a stay-at-home mom and a postal worker father. Tom was a C student in school, but he tried hard and was good to be around. While Jake's family was imploding after his mom's death, Hank's accident and Billie-Jack's inability to be a responsible parent, the Perkinses were the poster children for what a well-balanced, normal family looked like.

"I remember once," he said softly, and then sighed. "I'd been in a fight with Billie-Jack. I was, I don't know, about fourteen…that day the old man was picking on the twins for some reason of his own. I remember he'd taken the strap to Joss, and I said something to antagonize him so he'd switch his anger to me. I'd had a growth spurt that summer, so I was bigger and stronger. Billie-Jack gave me a black eye and a cut lip. I broke his nose." He paused, thinking of the violence of that time, wondering how they'd all pulled through so seemingly unscathed. Billie-Jack's rages were unpredictable, fueled by alcohol and memory of the wife he'd lost, and Jake always endeavored for those rages to be directed toward him and not the younger kids. "I went to Tom's that afternoon, and his mom patched me up. I can remember thinking, this is what a family should look like, this is how it should be. Thankfully, Billie-Jack was out of our lives a couple of years later."

"I remember that black eye," she said and met his gaze. "I was crushing on you back then and wanted to ask you about it. I'd heard the rumors, of course, about your dad, and knew your mom had passed away. You know, I used to envy the fact you had so many siblings...there seemed to be a Culhane in every grade at school. I guess we all wished for what we didn't have back then."

Jake raised a brow. "Except for Tom."

She shook her head. "He envied you."

"Why?" he asked incredulously.

"Because you were strong and fearless," she said simply. "Because you had the courage to fight for what was important to you. And then the courage to fight for your country. He always admired that about you, always bragged about his friend who wasn't afraid of anything."

"I didn't fight for us, though, did I?"

She shrugged. "I was so busy fighting *against* us, I don't think it would have mattered."

"I guess everything worked out as it should have," he remarked quietly. "You married Tom and had a great kid."

"I'm very grateful for T.J.," she said so softly he could barely hear her. "He's the most important thing in the world to me."

"I can see that. You're a wonderful mom, Abby."

"Jake, about T.J.," she said, her expression hauntingly vulnerable in that moment. "I know that you—"

"I'll make sure he's safe when we're snowboarding," he said, cutting her off. "If that's what you're concerned about. I wouldn't let anything happen to him."

"I know," she replied. "I trust you."

Something uncurled inside his chest, something that had everything to do with Abby knowing him and trusting him with what was most precious to her. And for some reason he couldn't fathom, she looked achingly vulnerable, as though she had the weight of the world pressing down on her narrow shoulders.

"Thank you for dinner," he said, figuring it was time to leave before he did something foolish—like kiss her.

"I should get going. I need to send off the proposal to O'Sullivan tonight."

"If you get the contract, does that mean you'll be staying in town a little longer?"

He shrugged, feeling the heat of her gaze through to his blood. "I don't usually get involved in the installation side of things. I'll hire contractors for that. I had planned on leaving after the wedding."

"That's next weekend, right?"

He nodded. "Best man duties. But Mitch has asked if I'll stay until after Christmas," he said and shrugged. "I'm not sure. So, I'll pick you up in the morning, around nine?" When she frowned, he quickly elaborated. "For your tree, remember. We promised your son."

She hesitated and then nodded. "Yes, of course."

Jake lingered by the counter for a moment and then pulled his keys from his jean pocket. "Good night, Abby."

"T.J. will want to say goodbye," she said and called her son.

Minutes later, Jake was at the front door, jacket on, helmet in his hand, promising T.J. he'd see him the following day. The child was beyond excited about the prospect of getting a Christmas tree. He noticed how they remained on the porch as he drove off, and he waved once he was down the street. By the time he was back at the hotel, the uneasy knot that had been gathering in his gut all evening gained momentum. He couldn't peg the cause and didn't imagine it was anything other than a simple reaction to spending time with Abby after so many years. But he couldn't be sure. Despite the feeling, being with Abby and her son had had an unusual effect on him. Because he liked hanging out with them. And it wasn't simply because he was still attracted to Abby. It wasn't about getting laid. Or even about mending fences or assuaging the guilt he felt for sleeping with her after Tom's death. It was the same thing it had always been—an unrelenting connection that went soul-deep. *Heart-deep*. She was the only woman he had ever loved.

And, he suspected, still did.

As promised, Jake arrived on her doorstep at nine o'clock the following morning. T.J., who had quickly decided Jake was *totally awesome*, was waiting on the porch, wearing his favorite overalls, rubber boots, gloves and an orange parka. Jake pulled up in a top-of-the-line Ranger, complete with a booster seat in the back, which she recognized as belonging to his brother Joss.

Abby ignored how good he looked in his jeans, black shirt and sheepskin lined aviator jacket. All her energy needed to go into telling Jake that T.J. was his son. She was a nervous wreck and he'd figure out why soon enough.

Where's my nerve gone?

It had spectacularly deserted her over the past week. But the more time Jake spent with T.J., the more opportunity he would have to put the math together and realize he was his son.

Guilt plagued her…and rightly so. For whatever her reasons for keeping his paternity a secret in the past, the fact that Jake was suddenly in the present should be all the motivation she needed to come clean.

And I will…but first, I want them to bond a little more.

It was about protecting T.J., about making sure that Jake had a real connection to him before she dropped the bombshell.

"Good morning," he said when he reached the gate.

While Abby locked the front door, T.J. was down the steps and through the gate, high-fiving the man he had assumed was her *new boyfriend*. Since male company was so lacking in her life, Abby wasn't surprised her inquisitive and highly intelligent son had come to that conclusion. Jake was the first man she'd invited to dinner in their home, the first man she'd consciously allowed T.J. to spend time with other than his teacher and coaches at school. She still considered him too young for sleepovers at the homes of his two closest school friends, although they had both asked. Besides, he could be willful and defiant at bedtime, and that wasn't something she wanted to force onto another unprepared parent while he was still so young. Maybe in a year or two, but for now, Abby was content to keep him close.

Except for the walking and talking complication of Jake Culhane!

"Hi," she said and headed down the path.

T.J. was quickly secured into the booster seat in the back, which they'd taken from her car, and he and Jake were chatting about something she couldn't hear. She pushed back her alarm and smiled when Jake opened the passenger door for her. She looked at her beaming son in the back seat, and her heart flipped over. He looked so happy—she could barely imagine how he would feel once he knew the truth about Jake. He'd be confused too, and rightly so. But Abby suspected happiness would override any other feelings. At least, that's what she hoped for.

They were on the road shortly after and headed to David McCall's ranch. Abby had met David many times and knew his son Jasper from the elementary school T.J. attended, although he was a couple of years older than her son. And, of course, he was her friend Annie's employer. The ranch wasn't as large as the Triple C, the big Culhane spread, but then, David wasn't exactly a rancher. He owned a very successful accounting practice in town, and his ranch was more like a hobby farm. The white gates were familiar, and she remembered Jake taking her to a few family gatherings on the ranch when they had been dating. Since then, and particularly since T.J. was born, Abby had managed to avoid any real interactions with the Culhanes or the McCalls. Her friendship with Annie was about as close as she got to the family.

Except for right now.

Once they pulled up, she noticed David striding from the stables, with Jasper close at hand. T.J. was out of the vehicle like the Flash, and she quickly followed suit, watching as David and Jake greeted one another with a handshake and laughter.

"Hey, Abby," David said and smiled. "Nice to see you."

"You, too," she said, watching discreetly as T.J. and Jasper hung out together by the corral. "Thank you for this. My son was convinced we'd never get a Christmas tree."

"There's plenty left to choose from," he said and jerked a thumb in the direction behind the main house. "Help yourself."

She smiled. "Is Annie around?"

He shook his head. "She's at the Triple C with Tess, doing some last-minute wedding stuff, I think." He looked toward Jake and chuckled. "I left a chain saw out for you. You sure you're not too much of a city boy to handle it?"

"I'm pretty sure I'll manage," Jake replied.

Minutes later they were all walking around the house, with both boys in their wake, with Jasper giving detailed advice on which tree he thought was the best. T.J., of course, had to inspect every one and finally settled on a lovely Black Hills spruce that would fit neatly into the corner of her living room.

"I love the scent of pine," she said and inhaled deeply.

Jake had the chain saw in his hand. "Is this the one?" he asked and gestured to the tree beside her.

She nodded and stepped back, and within seconds the chain saw roared. Soon after the tree tumbled while the two boys whooped and cheered on the sidelines and then yelled *timber*. Jake and David effortlessly dragged the tree back to the Ranger and tethered it quickly and securely to the tray.

"Mommy," T.J. said excitedly. "Can I go with Jasper and his dad to see his new fish tank?"

She unconsciously glanced toward Jake, seeking reassurance for a second, and then caught herself before he could realize. "Of course," she said quietly. "But only for a few minutes."

"Won't be long," David said and rounded up both boys, ushering them toward the house.

She watched, arms folded, as her son skipped away from her without a backward glance.

"We can go inside," Jake said from behind her. "If you're worried."

She turned, surprised to find him barely a foot away. "I'm not. I just…well, I suppose I am a little overprotective."

"Understandable," he said quietly. "But my cousin is a responsible parent, so he's quite safe."

"I know," she said and smiled tightly. "Habit. I've been the constant in his life for so long, although Gran keeps telling me I need to let go."

"I imagine it's hard being both mom and dad. He seems very well adjusted, though."

"He is," she replied proudly. "But he's also prone to temper tantrums when he doesn't get his own way. Which I'm sure you'll discover on the way home when he starts asking for a fish tank."

Jake chuckled. "He told me earlier that he wants a puppy."

"Or a kitten," she added and sighed. "Or a rabbit. I think he'd settle for a hamster at this point. But pets are a big commitment, and with my job and his schooling…finding the time for another thing to look after isn't on my radar."

He met her gaze. "Shall we take a walk?" he suggested, his eyes glittering with such raw intensity it knocked the breath from her lungs. "Check out the stables? If I remember correctly, you always had a thing for haylofts."

She colored hotly, remembering how they had played hooky one afternoon in senior year and spent a few hours in the stables at the Triple C, making out and then making love, before being caught by Mitch and the ranch foreman. They'd spent an embarrassing few minutes scampering back into clothes and pulling straw from their hair and then several more minutes explaining to Mitch why they weren't in school. Even though Mitch was only two years older, by then he was very much the father figure of the Culhane family and the glue that kept them all together.

Abby turned and headed for the stables, halting when she reached the door. The scent of sweet hay and horses assailed her immediately, and memory quickly bombarded her thoughts. During the time they had dated, the scents and sights of ranching life had become as familiar to her as the life she led with her mother and grandmother. She imagined her son living on a ranch, being a part of the legacy that was the Culhane family, and she knew she had denied him that opportunity. The guilt she felt intensified. As did the awareness she experienced whenever Jake was in her radius.

"Jake…"

He grasped her hand, and electricity shot up her arm as he led her farther into the stables. It was cold, but Abby was burning like a furnace, acutely aware of the way their fingers were linked.

"Abby." He said her name so softly she was compelled to move closer, as though his voice had a seductive power she couldn't refuse. "What are we doing?"

"Doing?"

His grip tightened. "Why did you invite me to dinner last night? And why did you come here today?"

"You asked me…" she said, her words trailing off.

"Exactly," he said and moved closer. "And you said yes."

"Because…because… I want…"

"A week ago you acted as though you couldn't bear to be in the same room with me. I'm leaving soon. And you and me…me and you…it's got train wreck written all over it. We both know that."

Tell him the truth…now.

She let out a shuddering breath and tried to get the words out. "I want… I want you to spend time with—"

"With you," he said, cutting her off. "I get that, Abby. I want that, too…even though I don't quite understand why. I mean, of course I know," he added and shook his head, moving her hand and holding it against his chest. "But we were kids back then. And what happened between us after Tom's funeral…we both agreed that was crazy and shouldn't have happened."

His words struck her down deep. Because saying it shouldn't have happened was like saying T.J. shouldn't exist. And that was unthinkable.

"I can't think that," she said, feeling him against her. "I did…once. But not now."

"What changed?" he asked, reaching for her chin and tilting her head up gently.

Abby met his gaze. "Everything."

"Everything?" he queried softly, his gaze moving to her mouth, and she knew exactly what he was thinking.

"You came back," she whispered. "You came home."

"Damn," he muttered and then he kissed her, his mouth touching hers so softly that she instinctively pushed forward, wanting more. It had been so long since she'd been kissed. So long since she'd felt the intimacy of breath against breath, of a man's arms holding her, of want and desire. Too long. She'd missed it. And this was Jake. Her first love. And suddenly, she couldn't resist. Couldn't deny. Couldn't forget how much she had once loved him.

His other hand moved along her back and rested on her hip as his mouth gently caressed hers. Abby's lips parted and his tongue slid inside, finding hers, entwining in a way that was achingly erotic, and she sighed low in her throat, quickly clutching for him, gripping his arms, curling her fingers around strong muscles. There was nothing else to do but *feel*. Nothing else to feel but the sweetness of his kiss, his touch, the sense that his soul was burning deeply into hers.

Finally, he dragged his mouth away and released her, steadying her as she stumbled.

"This isn't sensible, Abby," he said raggedly.

She uncurled her fingers and stepped back. "I know."

"So, we shouldn't."

She nodded. Of course, he was right. She shouldn't have lost her head. "You're right. It's just chemistry, I guess."

He didn't disagree and shrugged loosely. "I have a life in Sacramento. Like you have a life here. I don't want to confuse things for either of us. And if we got involved, things *would* be confused."

Abby wanted to shout out that he'd misunderstood her motives. *This isn't about us. This is about our son. Your son.*

"Sure."

He frowned. "Abby, don't be angry."

"I'm not," she said and peered over one of the stalls. A large gray horse swung its head over the door and whinnied softly. Although she'd always been nervous around horses, with Jake at her side she wasn't scared, so she stroked the animal's muzzle and sighed. "It was just a kiss, Jake. No big deal."

"Kissing you has always been a big deal, Abby," he said and moved up beside her, resting his forearms on the stall door. "That's the problem."

It was quite the revelation. But she knew there was truth in his words. Their attraction for one another had remained throughout the years, fueled by memory and the knowledge of things not done and words left unsaid.

"Why didn't you come back when I married Tom? I know he wanted you to be his best man."

"You know why," he replied. "Despite the fact we were over, I couldn't stand by and watch you marry my best friend."

She let out a long breath and turned, crossing her arms. "I think he knew that. You know, I did fall in love with him," she said and sighed. "He understood me. He knew what I was feeling back then, how I was still reeling from our breakup, and he still wanted to be with me. And later he wanted to marry me. He was content to stay in Cedar River and live a quiet life. A good life. One I don't regret."

"But?"

Of course there was a *but*. And they both knew it. She wondered how he could possibly know her so well, could sense her feelings in so many ways, and yet hadn't figured out the truth of T.J.'s paternity. *Blinded by what he doesn't want to see.* If Jake didn't want to be a father, what then? What would that mean for her son? The notion of her child being rejected wounded Abby to her very core. She needed time to think, to prepare herself for the inevitable disappointment. It wasn't as though Jake had proven himself to be some kind of family man, after all. He rarely returned to Cedar River to see his siblings. Perhaps he wasn't wired that way. Not everyone was made to be a parent or to care deeply for family.

"But sometimes I wonder," she said quietly. "What might have happened if you hadn't joined the military. Or if I'd been a little more…flexible."

"Do you mean would we have stayed together?" He shrugged, but his shoulders were tight. "The advantage of youth is being filled with optimism and a sense of invincibility. Back then I thought we were strong enough to get through anything. But neither of us was prepared to compromise."

He was right. They had both been stubborn and uncompromising back then. "I know you're leaving soon, Jake, and going back to Sacramento. But…and I know you might not understand why, but I want us to be friends. It's important to me. And last week, you said that's what you wanted, too."

"I do," he remarked. "I've never liked the idea of you being out there and hating me, Abby. It didn't seem right, somehow."

"Let's make a promise," she said and held out her hand. "We'll always be friends, no matter what?"

He took her hand, intimately linking their fingertips. "No matter what."

Abby wanted to believe him, wanted to think they would be able to maintain a friendly relationship once he knew the truth about T.J., but she wasn't sure.

One thing she did know—her time was running out.

Chapter Seven

As Jake watched Abby and her son decorate the Christmas tree later that morning, it occurred to him that with every hour he spent in their company, the deeper he was getting involved. And the damnable thing was, he enjoyed hanging out with them. Despite the attraction that fired through his blood, despite wanting to kiss her again as he'd done in the stables, he *liked* Abby. As much as he always had. She was easy to be around, easy to talk to about mundane and everyday things. And he liked her kid, too.

It made him wonder. About family. About what kind of husband and father he would make some day. Faithful, for sure. And protective. The more he thought about it, the more agreeable the notion became. He considered some of the women he'd dated back in Sacramento, realizing that none of them seemed particularly maternal, and then laughed to himself because he figured he knew absolutely *nothing* about the goings-on of the female psyche.

"Did you say something?" she asked as she draped a tinsel garland around the tree.

Jake was sitting on the sofa, feeling absurdly relaxed, watching T.J.'s animated expression as he played with the Christmas baubles before handing them to his mother. "The tree looks good."

She planted her hands on her hips. "Yes, it's a masterpiece."

Jake's gaze wandered to the mantel above the fireplace.

He spotted Tom's picture, and regret and guilt kicked in. He couldn't help wondering what his friend would think of him being back in Cedar River *and* back in Abby's life.

Not back, he corrected. *Just passing through.*

"*That's* my angel daddy," T.J. said and pointed to the picture, clearly noticing Jake's attention to the photograph.

"I know," Jake remarked and saw yearning in the child's eyes. "He would have been very proud of you."

T.J.'s chest puffed out. "He had red hair," he said and grinned. "But I've got brown hair like Mommy."

In fact, the child's hair was darker than his mother's, and his eyes were green, not blue like Abby's. For the life of him, Jake couldn't recall the color of Tom's eyes. Obviously green, like the little boy in front of him.

"Are you staying for lunch?" Abby asked, abruptly changing the subject.

Jake's brows shot up. "Am I invited?"

She nodded—a little warily, he thought. "Sure."

He did stay, enjoying a relaxed hour over sandwiches and leftover cider, with T.J. insisting he wanted a fish, a puppy *and* a kitten for Christmas, and with Abby nodding appropriately. The more time he spent with them, the more he realized how much of a handful the child could be. He was smart and inquisitive about anything and everything and had a defiant streak, often pushing his mother's buttons with unreasonable demands on her time and attention. Abby, however, was amazingly patient and generally managed to defuse her son's tantrums. Like when she told him to wash up after lunch, he wailed something about not liking the soap in the bathroom. Jake stayed out of it, figuring it wasn't any of his concern or business. But he felt for Abby, having to be both parents to an obviously demanding little boy.

It was around two o'clock when he finally left, with

the promise to see them the following day, and headed to Joss's place. His brother only lived a few streets away, and when he pulled up outside the large craftsman-style home, his nieces came racing down the front path, calling him Uncle Jake and clearly delighted to see him. It was a strange reality, and one he realized he was beginning to get used to. Family had come easily to both Joss and Mitch, and he knew his nieces adored Hank. Even workaholic Grant was more involved in the girls' lives than he was. But over the course of the last few weeks, Jake had experienced a shift in his relationship with his family. Being *present* in their lives had given them, and him, an opportunity to get acquainted as he never had before. For the first time in forever, Cedar River almost felt like *home*.

Of course, he knew it wasn't permanent. His life, friends and work were in Sacramento, but he was committed to returning more often—maybe even regularly.

"Your keys," he said to his brother as he met Joss on the porch, and held out the Ranger's key ring. "Thanks for the loan."

Joss's mouth curled. "You may as well keep them, since you need the truck for your snowboarding adventure tomorrow."

Jake shrugged. "I'll come by in the morning and grab them. You might need the truck tonight."

His brother's expression was instantly curious. "What's gotten into you? You're so friendly and accommodating these days."

He quickly read between the lines of Joss's comment. "You have something to say?"

"How was your date last night?"

He nodded. "Fine. Although I'm not sure it was a date."

"And today?" Joss probed.

"She needed a Christmas tree," he explained and waved a hand vaguely. "That's all."

Joss raised a disbelieving brow. "You're so full of crap. You've been spending a lot of time with Abby lately. And her kid."

Jake shrugged loosely. "I'm sure you have a point to make?"

Joss shook his head. "No point. Just…be careful. You bringing her to the wedding?"

"I hadn't planned on it."

Joss chuckled. "So, you wouldn't mind if *I* ask her out?" his brother queried. "I mean, she's pretty as hell, a single mom, I'm a single dad…it has all the makings of a perfect match."

Jake's gut clenched and he scowled, propping his hands on his hips. "Seriously? You want to *date* Abby?"

"No," Joss replied and grinned broadly. "I only wanted to see if you'd look like you wanted to punch me in the teeth at the idea."

Jake shook his head and made an impatient sound. "You're such a horse's ass. And my least favorite brother."

Joss laughed. "Ah, where's your sense of humor? You *should* ask Abby to the wedding."

He wasn't about to admit he'd fleetingly thought about it. "We'll see."

"It's not like you're leaving straight away, right?" Joss suggested. "Mitch said you were staying on until after the new year?"

He nodded. "Most likely."

"You know, you're welcome to stay here," his brother said and grinned again. "There's plenty of room, and the girls seem to like having their usually absent uncle around. Might give you a chance to get to know them better. Unless there's a particular reason you prefer the hotel?"

"No reason," Jake replied. "Simply convenient."

Which of course wasn't entirely true. Joss's home was equally as convenient. Only, being at the hotel meant he had the opportunity to see Abby when she was working. Plus, he had the business proposal for O'Sullivan under consideration. It made sense to stay in town.

He hung out with his brother for a while, avoiding the subject of Abby and her son whenever Joss mentioned them. He was back at the hotel by four, ordered room service, spoke to his business partner at length around five o'clock, watched a little television and had an early night. Sleep would have been great, but he spent most of the time staring at the ceiling or the digital clock on the bedside table.

It was after ten when he showed up at Abby's the following morning, after detouring to Joss's to collect the Ranger and snowboarding gear. T.J., as expected, was waiting for him on the porch, outfitted in his snow gear and clearly excited by the prospect of their snowboarding expedition.

"He's hardly slept," Abby said as she greeted him by the door, looking beautiful in jeans, knee-high boots, a sweater and a bright pink jacket with faux fur around the hood and cuffs.

"You look pretty," he said and stared at her.

She smiled. "Thank you."

"I was wondering," he said and held out a vague hand. "If you'd like to come with me to Mitch and Tess's wedding on Saturday? It's only a small gathering at the ranch, just family and a few friends. Not too formal."

She took a step backward. "Ah…like your date?"

"*As* my date," he said and nodded.

"Can I come, too?"

T.J.'s query made him smile. "Of course," he replied and grinned in the child's direction. "My nieces and Jasper will be there, too. But first, see if you can get your mommy to say yes."

"Say yes, Mommy!" T.J. insisted and whooped around the porch. "Please."

Jake waited for her response, experiencing an unusual case of nerves, almost as though he was sixteen again and asking her out for the first time.

"Unless you don't like weddings?" he teased.

"I like weddings. Okay," she said softly. "I'll go."

"*We'll* go," T.J. corrected cheerfully. "And now can we go snowboarding?"

"We sure can, buddy," he replied, ignoring the twitch behind his ribs that felt a whole lot like a foolish kind of happiness. He didn't overthink it, didn't try to reason himself out of it. "Let's go."

"That's a nice dress."

Abby smoothed the blue fabric over her hips and smiled. "Thanks, Gran."

"So, have you decided when you're going to tell Jake about T.J.?"

"Gran, shush," she said and frowned, darting a glance toward the doorway. "T.J. might hear you."

"He's too busy checking his bag for his sleepover at the ranch on Saturday," Patience said, her silvery brows regarding her questioningly. "Which I'm stunned to discover you agreed to."

Abby expelled a heavy breath. "All the kids are staying over after the wedding."

"All?"

"Joss's girls and David's two kids," she explained.

"Annie and Ellie are going to be watching them. He'll be perfectly safe."

"I don't doubt it," her grandmother replied. "I'm just surprised you agreed."

She briefly explained how the invitation had come about when she bumped into Ellie and Jake at the hotel the day before. Jake had mentioned it, and then Ellie quickly offered for T.J. to stay over once the bride and groom left for the evening. When she ran the idea by her son, he was over the moon at the prospect. She'd stay, of course, to ensure he was settled. And then decide if he was capable of spending a whole night with someone other than herself or her grandmother.

"I think it will be good for him. And you're always telling me I need to stop being so overprotective," she reminded Patience.

"I also say you should tell Jake the truth, but that doesn't seem to make any difference."

Abby sighed. "I'm going to tell him soon."

"At the wedding?" her grandmother asked incredulously.

"No," she replied. "After. I think that's best. Once I see how Jake behaves with his family and how T.J. interacts with them."

"Be careful, Abby," her grandmother warned. "Once you set yourself up as judge and jury, there's no going back."

Abby heard her grandmother's words but knew she had to do what felt right for her son. The truth was, she *had* put Jake to the fatherhood test for the past two weeks. And he had passed with flying colors. The snowboarding lesson was a huge success, which was followed by lunch at JoJo's Pizza Parlor. Later that afternoon, once they were back home, she watched while Jake listened attentively as T.J. read a story from his favorite book, and then they played a video game for a while. Jake was amazingly patient and considerate toward her son, and with each interaction, she felt less concerned and more convinced that he would step up and be the father that T.J. so desperately longed for. Her son, of course, had quickly developed a serious case of hero worship for Jake, and she could only imagine how happy he would be when he learned that he was his father.

Her own relationship with Jake was what concerned her. Because sex was raging between them like a red flag to a bull. Oh, he hadn't touched her. Hadn't kissed her since the time in the stables at the McCall ranch. Hadn't done anything to suggest he wanted to do any of those things. But she knew. The attraction and awareness between them was undeniable. It was in the looks they shared. The heat that seemed to flare up whenever they occupied the same space. Since she'd been working the lunch shift that week, he'd dropped by to see her every day. The first time it had been under the guise of the contract he'd successfully obtained to install the new security system at the hotel. The second time he didn't give any reason at all. And the third time she was waiting for him with coffee and cake once her shift had ended.

"I have to get to work," Abby said when she returned to the kitchen after slipping off the dress and hanging it in the closet. "I'll see you late this afternoon."

Patience nodded. "I'll pick T.J. up from school. You know," her grandmother said as she stirred the tea she'd just made, "all T.J. talks about these days is Jake. If you're not careful he'll work it out for himself…you know that's true."

"He still believes Tom is his father," she said quietly.

"For now. But the more time Jake spends with him, the

more questions he'll have. He told me you said he'd have a *real* father one day," Patience said and sighed. "You can't let him believe in a half-truth, Abby.

"I know, Gran."

"It's time."

"I know," she admitted, stronger this time. "And I *will* tell Jake. And T.J. I know T.J. wants a father and I think Jake will step up."

"And what about you and Jake?"

She shrugged. "Time will tell, I suppose."

"Do you think there's a chance you'll reconcile?"

Abby sighed. "Honestly, I don't know. We'll see what happens after Saturday."

Because Saturday night they had a date.

And after the wedding she was going to tell him he had a son.

She drove herself to the ranch Saturday afternoon, with an animated T.J. in the back seat, talking about how he couldn't wait to see the horses and cows and to hang out with the other children. The conversation made her realize how much her son longed for more company his own age. He had several friends at school, but other than soccer, he didn't do any other activity that would bring him into contact with other children. Because he was so academically advanced for his age, Abby always ensured he had books and his computer and art supplies, but he rarely had the chance to play games with other kids. She'd neglected that part of his education and planned on rectifying the oversight.

Jake greeted them when they pulled up in the driveway and immediately complimented her on her gown. But she was so dumbstruck by how gorgeous he looked in his gray suit, white shirt, bolo tie and Stetson that she could barely articulate a reply.

"Thank you for coming today," he said softly.

"Thank you for inviting me. I like weddings," she said with a sigh. "I always enjoy the event planning at the hotel, particularly the birthdays and weddings."

He smiled, and her heart flipped over. "Maybe you'll have another one someday."

"Maybe."

The wedding, as expected, was a lovely affair. Tess and Mitch looked so happy and so in love, she couldn't help feeling a little envious. Okay, a lot envious. With about twenty-five people in attendance, the ceremony was intimate and heartfelt, and she swallowed back the heat in her throat when the groom spoke vows about loving and protecting his bride and the child they were soon going to bring into the world. And it made her long for that same kind of love and connection. Afterward, there were toasts and food and soft music playing in the background. The kids were rounded up and kept entertained in the family room while the adults remained in the huge front living room. And if any of the Culhanes were surprised that she was attending, none made comment. Except for Annie, and since she wasn't a Culhane but a friend, Abby took her questions with a patient smile.

"Are you guys dating again?"

"Not exactly," she said and shrugged lightly. "It's complicated."

"Love usually is," Annie remarked.

Abby didn't bother with denials. Instead, she looked across the room and spotted Jake talking with his sister and David. T.J. wasn't too far away, hanging out with David's son and clearly delighted to be a part of things. And again it struck Abby how much T.J. looked like Jake and she couldn't believe that no one had ever questioned her about her son's paternity. The room was filled with Jake's family and, by extension, T.J.'s family. Surely one of them could see the truth she'd been hiding?

"What's going on with you, Abby?"

She looked back at her friend and saw Annie's concerned expression. She briefly touched the other woman's arm and spoke. "Ask me again the next time we catch up."

"You're being very mysterious."

She shook her head. "Just planning on making things right. Shall we get some cake?"

"Maybe later," Annie replied. "I need to check on the kids. Talk soon."

As her friend disappeared through the crowd Abby headed for the buffet table and perused the selection of cakes and desserts.

"Having fun?"

Jake had sidled up beside her and passed her a flute of champagne. "Yes. You?"

"Of course."

She clinked his glass. "You gave a good speech."

He shrugged loosely and gave her a lopsided grin. "Best man, you know."

"I've never thought anything different," she said softly. "You look nice in that outfit. Very urban cowboyish."

He placed a hand at the small of her back and leaned close. "You're so beautiful."

The scent of his cologne assailed her senses. "They look happy," she said, trying to ignore the way her heart fluttered, and gestured to the bride and groom, who were standing together by the fireplace, clearly oblivious to the fuss going on around them.

"Jealous?"

She met his gaze. "A little. This is exactly how I imagined a wedding should be…family and friends and an abundance of love."

"Like yours and Tom's?"

He was so close she could see the brilliance of his eyes clearly, and she shook her head. "I threw up twenty minutes before the ceremony. Nerves, I guess. But I don't think I have ever looked or been *that* happy," she said about the bride and groom and then exhaled. "Except, of course, when T.J. was born. He was a precious gift."

"If you're worried about him staying here tonight," he said, his gaze narrowing, "I'm sure you could—"

"I'm not," she assured him. "I know Ellie and Annie will look after him. And Joss offered to drop him at home when he picks the girls up."

"I didn't realize you and my brother were so well acquainted."

Abby smiled to herself, thinking he actually sounded jealous. "We see each other at school pickup sometimes. Actually, I bumped into him the other day, which was when he offered to bring T.J. home from the sleepover."

"Did he make a pass?" he asked, looking serious.

So he *was* jealous. "Not at all."

"Good," he replied and rested his hand possessively on her hip. "Because he's on his way over, and otherwise I might have to wrestle him to save your honor."

She chuckled. "My honor is intact," she assured him. "He's nowhere near as charming as he likes to make out."

Jake laughed. "That's so true. But it was nice of him to offer to drive T.J. home."

She nodded. "It's all part of my learning to let go and to stop being an overprotective mother. This is phase one. Phase two will be summer camp. By the time I get to phase one hundred, I'll be ready for him to go to college," she said and smiled. "Have I convinced you I'm okay with this?"

He bent his head and spoke close to her ear. "Almost."

"Hey, kids," Joss said cheerfully when he reached them. "Is all this marital bliss giving anyone any ideas?"

"Idiot," Jake muttered. "Haven't you got anywhere else to be?"

Joss laughed. "Nope," he said and came around to Abby's other side. "I just stopped by to assure you that I will get T.J. home tomorrow safe and sound. I'll take care of him as though he's one of my own," he said, and his voice suddenly dropped several octaves so that only *she* could hear. "Or at least," he said and winked at her, "like he's a very close relative."

Abby almost spluttered the champagne across the room.

He knows!

How *could* he know? And then she remembered all the times she'd seen him at school pickup and how often he'd nod in her direction. He'd clearly seen the resemblance between her son and his brother and he must have worked it out. He obviously hadn't said anything to Jake, and she couldn't imagine why. She tried desperately to avoid Joss's gaze, wanting to clamp her hands over her ears as he made small talk for a couple of minutes. She was relieved when he moved off to speak with his sister.

"Are you okay?" Jake asked. "You look pale."

"I'm fine," she lied. "I think I simply need some fresh air."

Jake nodded and grabbed her hand. "Come with me."

Moments later, they were walking down the hall. He stopped by the front door to grab her shawl and slipped it over her shoulders as they headed out on the porch, suddenly very much alone. The sounds of music, clinking dinnerware and laughter were muted once Jake shut the front door. He still hadn't relinquished her hand, and Abby was about to pull away when he drew her closer. She didn't resist, didn't do anything other than feel his strong body pressed to hers. He was aroused, but she didn't feel threatened. She looked up, both startled and overwhelmed by the desire she saw in his expression.

There it is…

Sex. Attraction. Chemistry. The things that had always bound her to Jake. And still did.

"Jake…"

"I wish I could control this feeling I have for you, Abby," he admitted, his voice raw. "But I can't."

"Me, either," she said on whisper.

Abby moved, arching against him, inviting the kiss she knew was inevitable. And wasn't disappointed. His mouth was on hers within seconds. His strong hands were at her waist. And his kiss was hot and erotic and blew her mind. Abby thrust her hands in his hair, shuddering, feeling him hard against her and wanting exactly what he was giving her. Somewhere, in a place that was about good sense and control, a tiny voice warned her not to get carried away. But she didn't listen. Didn't do anything other than *feel* him. He wanted her. She wanted him, and since she wasn't sure what tomorrow would bring, Abby knew exactly what she wanted.

"Make love to me," she muttered against his mouth, her tongue rasping his. "Tonight. Please."

He dragged his mouth away from hers and gently grabbed her shoulders, staring down into her face, his green eyes glittering with such burning and aroused intensity it rocked her to the core.

"I thought that was against the rules?" he said raggedly. "We're only going to be friends, remember?"

Abby shrugged. "Tonight, I don't care about rules. I only want to feel."

"And in the morning?"

She shrugged again and shivered. "We'll worry about that tomorrow."

Jake was out of his jacket within seconds and draped the garment around her shoulders. The warmth of the fabric enveloped her instantly, and she realized that was exactly how Jake had always made her feel—as though his arms were a warm and protective coat. When they broke up after graduation, that warmth and protection disappeared from her life. She'd tried to recapture it with Tom, but her husband, a man she genuinely *had* loved, had never made her feel the way Jake Culhane did.

They stayed out on the porch for a while, swaying to the faint sound of music coming from inside. There was an intense intimacy about the mood between them, as though they both knew the dancing was a prelude to something else, something more. By nine o'clock, the guests began leaving. The bride and groom also bailed and headed to the O'Sullivans' hotel for the night, and Abby had to make a decision about leaving T.J. at the ranch. The decision was made for her when her son wailed loudly, demanding to stay with his newfound friends. *Cousins.* But of course, no one knew that. No one except, she suspected, Joss. Who clearly and thankfully hadn't said anything to his brother. Or to her. But she knew he would at some point, which made Abby's need to tell Jake the truth all the more urgent. She hugged her son and left the ranch at nine forty-five. It was past ten when she arrived home. And nearly eleven when she heard the familiar rumble of Jake's motorbike in her driveway.

He didn't say a word when he crossed the threshold. He dumped his helmet, leather jacket and gloves on the hall stand, closed the door, and grabbed her hand, bringing her knuckles to his mouth and kissing them gently.

Abby led him down the hall and into her bedroom. Her

safe place. She flicked on the bedside light, slid out of her shoes and curled her toes into the carpet. He ditched his suit jacket and tie and placed them on the chair by the door. Boots and socks were next. Then his shirt. He was so spectacularly well cut and muscled; his chest was smattered with hair, his shoulders wide, his arms strong. He was perfectly proportioned and exactly as she remembered.

He extracted contraception from his wallet and dropped it onto the bedside table. Last time, the protection had failed. This time, she almost wished for the same thing, as the thought of having another child with Jake filled her with an inexplicable warmth. Of course, it wasn't the time to think of that. Another unplanned pregnancy wasn't on her radar. But one day…one day she would very much like to give her son a brother or sister.

"Come here, Abby," Jake said softly, his voice like a sexy caress.

She walked toward him, placing her hands on his hips, looking up into his eyes. "I'm here."

He undid the clip holding up her hair, and her tresses tumbled over her shoulders. "I've been wanting to do that all night," he admitted.

Abby sighed and smiled. "What else would you like to do?"

"Everything," he replied and lowered his head, taking her mouth in a scorching-hot kiss.

They were on the bed in seconds, naked barely moments after that. Even though there was nothing new to encounter, even though they had been together before and knew each other's bodies intimately, there was still a sense of newness, of discovery. When he touched her breasts, when he kissed her there, when he caressed her aching nipples with his tongue and she arched wildly against him,

Abby was lost in the sweet oblivion she'd craved from the moment he'd returned to town. And then he did more. He touched her, stroked her in the most sensitive places; he drew her higher and higher toward release. He trailed kisses down her rib cage, along her belly, lingering at the row of faded stretch marks that hadn't been there the last time they were together. She moved to cover herself, but he gently pushed her hand away.

"Don't," he said against her skin, kissing her belly softly. "You're beautiful, Abby."

With Jake, she had always felt beautiful. There was something in his touch, a kind of reverence, a hypnotic eroticism she'd not found before or since. And when he kissed her intimately, she was utterly lost. His hands gently caressed her breasts, his mouth lingering on her center, taking her on a journey of mind-blowing pleasure that defied belief.

And touching him had its own reward. She reacquainted herself with the things he liked, quickly remembering that she could make him crazy by kissing his neck, or stroking the smooth skin below his rib cage, or running her tongue around the edge of his navel. As much as he was the expert in making her reach the peak of pleasure, Abby knew she had the same power over him.

When he moved over her, finding her warm and ready, she stared into his eyes, not wanting to lose the erotic and powerful connection. Being with Jake, feeling him inside her, urging his hips to move with hers, was a powerful aphrodisiac. They climbed the peak together, and when she felt him shudder, when she felt his strong body shake with release, Abby held him tightly, letting pleasure claim them both.

Afterward, once their breathing returned to normal, he rolled onto his side, quickly disappearing into her master bathroom for a few moments to discard the condom. When he returned, Abby was lying on her side, the duvet mostly covering her nakedness. He was still half-aroused and moved around her bed without any kind of modesty. Abby smiled, moistening her lips as she pushed back the duvet to invite him back into her bed.

"Are you sleepy?" she asked as he moved alongside her.

He traced a fingertip along her arm. "Not particularly. You?"

She chuckled, feeling young and uninhibited and totally at ease, and then looked a little more somber. "No."

"But?"

The fact he knew her so well terrified her. "But I think we should talk."

His gaze narrowed a fraction. "Serious talk?"

Abby nodded. "About…about T.J."

He grasped her chin and held her face steady. "I get it, Abby. I understand that you're a single mom and have to put him first. I've never dated anyone with kids before," he admitted and then shrugged a little. "I mean, not that we're *dating*. But we're *something*…and that makes things complicated. I don't want to mislead you, Abby, and I certainly didn't come back with any intention of reconnecting or revisiting our past relationship. But we did—we have," he added and kissed her mouth softly. "And I'm not sorry. I can't regret being with you like this. Can you?"

She swallowed hard. "No, but T.J.—"

"Is your priority," he said and nodded. "I know. As he should be."

The truth teetered on the edge of her tongue. Damn him for being so understanding. Damn him for having such a tender touch, such a mind-blowing kiss.

And damn him for still being the love of my life…

The realization that she still loved him, *had never*

stopped loving him, shook Abby to her deepest core. She knew she was in way over her head. They'd made love and it had been incredible, but the reality of their situation pressed down on her like a lead weight. Once she told him about T.J., she knew things would change. Right now, in the moment, their relationship was about *them*. About sex and passion and the possibility of rekindling old feelings. He was considerate of her son, aware that having a relationship with someone who had a child was complex and required certain agreements. And he had openly admitted to never having dated anyone who had children. But once he knew T.J. was his son, Abby suspected everything would change. She wouldn't be able to live in the sudden romantic bubble they were now in. Real life would intrude.

And it scared her to pieces. Because she knew what it would mean.

I'll lose him again...

Which was an unbearable thought. And her courage dwindled. Tomorrow, she thought when he kissed her again. *I'll tell him tomorrow.*

And tomorrow, she discovered, came way too soon. They slept some, in between making love again, talking and reminiscing about days gone by. They didn't mention Tom or T.J., but she spoke about her mother and grandmother. And she talked about her father and what not having him in her life had meant to her. They talked a little about their past, reminiscing about high school, about the happy days. Jake said a few things about his family and his time in the military and how he had settled back into civilian life way easier than he'd imagined. He told her about some of his friends who hadn't made it home, and she heard real pain in his voice. He talked about loss, about how so many of his platoon had struggled with PTSD when they'd returned from active duty. He admitted he'd visited a veterans' support group a few times. As he talked, Abby listened, thinking they'd never been closer or more connected than they were in those few stolen hours. And she wanted to hold on to it, to keep the moment close to her heart.

"I was so scared for you," she admitted, touching his face. "I used to light a candle every Sunday when you were overseas, as a way to protect you. Silly," she said and traced his jawline, feeling the sexy stubble.

"It worked," he said, grasping her hand and holding it against his heart. "I came back."

"Tom always knew. He never said anything, never asked me not to. He wanted you to be safe, too."

"I know. He was a good person." Jake kissed her knuckles. "It's sad to think he never got to meet his son."

Tell him...

Abby's breath caught in her throat. "Jake, I—"

"I've missed you, Abby," he said huskily and kissed her mouth. "I've missed this."

The kiss deepened and she was lost, quickly caught up in the passion only he could make her feel. They made love again, a slow and gentle coupling that left her mindless. Jake wrung every ounce of pleasure from her, giving and taking, possessing her in a way that was almost otherworldly and cemented what she already knew—she was still completely and totally in love with him.

When the sun rose, they made out for a while, then showered together, and Abby made him French toast for breakfast. They ate and drank coffee and she marveled at how easy it was to have him in her kitchen. The mood between them was relaxed and intimate, and she had almost worked herself into having the courage to come clean about T.J. when her cell pinged and she read a message from Annie saying that Joss was on his way with the kids.

"Your brother will be here soon," she said, replying to the text with a thumbs-up emoji.

Jake was by the kitchen counter, sipping coffee. "Do you want me to leave?"

She shook her head. There was no point in being coy or secretive about their relationship or the fact he'd spent the night. "No. We really need to talk."

"More talk?" he queried and snatched her hand, hauling her close and then kissing her soundly. They kissed for a while, which was crazy, she knew, because they has so much to discuss. But being in his arms was like a tonic, and she needed it to soothe the uneasiness searing through to her soul. "What's going on in that beautiful head of yours?" he asked when they finally stopped kissing.

"So much," she admitted, and her eyes burned. "I'm so sorry, Jake."

His gaze narrowed and he tilted her chin, searching her face. "For what?"

Before she could reply, they heard a car pull up outside, and within minutes there were feet stomping on the porch. Abby was quickly at the front door, and seconds later her son flung himself at her legs.

"Mommy!" he announced excitedly. "I'm home."

"So I see. I missed you."

"I missed you more!"

Joss's daughters followed him inside, and Abby invited Jake's brother across the threshold and into the kitchen. If Joss thought it was strange to see Jake sitting at the big scrubbed table, drinking coffee, wearing most of the same suit he'd worn the night before, he gave a good impression of acting as though it were an everyday occurrence. And Abby was so wound up she didn't have the strength to overthink the situation. T.J. dumped his knapsack on the table and unzipped his sweater, and she spotted a large stain down the front of his T-shirt.

"A slight mishap with a container of chocolate chip ice cream this morning, I believe," Joss said and laughed, ushering his daughters to stay by his side.

Abby made a face and regarded her son. "You ate ice cream for breakfast?"

T.J. shrugged. "I was hungry, Mommy. I found it in the freezer. They got a freezer that's as big as a house," he added dramatically. "I didn't get in trouble. Ellie said she eats ice cream for breakfast, too, sometimes."

She couldn't be angry with him, since he looked so adorable with the remnants of chocolate on his face, his green eyes filled with excitement. He'd clearly had a fabulous time at the ranch.

With his family...

Abby looked toward Jake, saw that he was watching them, then she glanced at Joss, wishing the other man would leave so she could come clean and tell Jake the truth. Or maybe she was hoping that Joss would announce the obvious and she'd be off the hook—which made her feel like the greatest coward of all time. She shook off her cowardice, determined that once Joss left, she would tell Jake the truth. But then T.J., her beautiful and amazing son, unexpectedly pulled off his soiled shirt, struggling with the neck, giggling and laughing, oblivious to the chain of events he was about to set off.

Because there, on his small shoulder, for everyone to see, was the lightning-bolt birthmark that clearly branded him as Jake's son.

Chapter Eight

Jake wasn't sure how long it took him to get to his feet. One second? Two? Not long. Long enough for him to hear Abby's startled gasp, for him to see the concerned look on his brother's face.

The birthmark.

He knew it well. He had one in the same spot. In the same shape.

It was an impossible coincidence.

Oh my freaking god.

He quickly registered the sudden terror in Abby's expression, and for a few excruciating seconds he couldn't breathe, couldn't think, couldn't move. He simply stared. At T.J. Then at Abby. Into Abby. And he knew, without a doubt, exactly what he was seeing. And what he *hadn't* seen for the last couple of weeks.

The truth.

He heard Abby's voice, registered she was instructing T.J. to put his sweater back on.

"Joss," he heard her say over the white noise that was now screeching through his eardrums. "Could you take T.J. next door to my grandmother's house? Your brother and I need to talk."

"Yeah…sure," Joss replied with a heavy sigh.

"But I wanna stay here, Mommy," T.J. wailed. "With you and Jake."

"Come on, kiddo," Joss said and quickly ushered the

kids together, including T.J. "You can tell your grand-mother all about the ice cream you ate for breakfast."

"Great-Gran makes me eat oatmeal."

"I'll tell you a secret," Joss said and managed to smile despite the chaos in the room. "I think oatmeal tastes like rubber. So how about we go now?"

Jake watched as T.J. resisted for a moment but then agreed. Jake caught his brother's stare, saw sympathy and acknowledgment—as though his brother knew exactly what was happening, but couldn't muster the strength to respond. He could only stare at Abby.

Once the room was cleared and the definitive sound of the door closing made its way to his ears, Jake faced her squarely, his rage and confusion rising and gathering momentum with every passing second. "One question."

"Yes," she said simply.

"Yes?" he barked back instantly.

"Yes," she said again. "He's your son."

Jake grabbed the edge of the table, watching his fingers turn white as his grip tightened. Fury and disbelief churned through his blood, across his skin, into every cell he possessed. He swallowed hard, his throat aching, trying to form words. Finally, he managed to say something. "How is that possible?"

She sucked in a breath. "I got pregnant that afternoon we spent together."

"The math doesn't add up," he reminded her harshly. "Tom's funeral was in September. T.J. was born in March. That's seven months."

"He was premature," she said quietly, twisting her hands together. "Almost seven weeks."

Jake's temple throbbed. "He's not Tom's child?"

"No," she replied.

"You're sure?"

"Positive," she said and nodded. "Tom had a very low sperm count. We'd tried conceiving and it never happened. We were talking about using a sperm donor when he got sick. He's not Tom's, Jake. He's yours."

Jake straightened, filled his lungs with air and glared at her. "He's mine. You've just been passing him off as Tom Perkins's son for the last six years, then?"

She didn't deny it. Instead, she shrugged and moved across the room, her back to him, her arms crossed, her head held at a tight angle. A mix of feelings raced through him, crawling across his skin. The white noise increased, deafening him, becoming the only sound he heard as he endeavored to understand what was happening.

I have a son...

Every ounce of self-control, every sense Jake possessed of knowing exactly who and what he was, suddenly and spectacularly disappeared, abandoning him when he needed it the most. He'd always counted on knowing he could rely on his instincts. As an adolescent dealing with Billie-Jack's drunkenness, he would antagonize the old man to keep his fists away from his siblings. As a soldier, he valued the job he was doing, showing courage under fire, being the best version of himself he could be. As a civilian, he worked hard to be successful, to be a valuable contributor to society, to make good choices. And as a man, he always treated people fairly and with respect. He never made promises he couldn't keep. He never lied. And now, faced with the biggest lie he had ever been told, Jake didn't know how he should feel. Or what he should think. Or, more importantly, what he should do.

"He doesn't know?" Jake asked quietly, fighting the rage and the helplessness seeping through his blood and into his bones.

She turned, facing him, her eyes glistening. "No." Then she shuddered. "I had planned on telling him."

Jake digested the information. "When?"

"Soon. After I told you."

Jake was so overwhelmed he could barely draw a breath. "Who knows the truth?"

She swallowed hard. "My grandmother. My mom. My best friend, Renee. And…I think Joss knows."

"You *think*?"

"He said something at the wedding…and just now, he didn't exactly looked surprised. I'm not sure…perhaps he just suspected."

Jake felt as though his head was about to explode. If his brother suspected it, surely he would have said something? "What about Tom's parents?"

She nodded and shrugged. "They never asked who his father was, but I think they guessed. They knew about Tom's fertility issues."

"Is that why they left town?"

"I think so. There was nothing left here for them after Tom died. And once I came back to town with T.J.," she said and sighed. "They kept their distance, and a few months later they left."

"Came back from where?" he demanded.

"Denver," she replied. "When I realized I was pregnant, I visited Renee, to refocus and make a few decisions."

"One of them *not* being to let me know you were having my baby?" he shot back, so angry, so filled with disbelief he could taste the betrayal in his mouth.

"You were back in a war zone," she replied. "I didn't know how to—"

"Any one of my brothers could have contacted me," he said harshly.

"I know that," she admitted. "But frankly, at first I was just so shocked to learn I was pregnant. Along with the grief of Tom's death, I shut down, I guess. And then T.J. arrived early, and those first few weeks were so incredibly hard. He was so tiny and I didn't know if he was going to make it and all my concentration was put into him getting well and I couldn't—"

"It didn't occur to you that I had a *right* to be there when our child was fighting for his life?" he demanded, running a frustrated hand through his hair.

"Of course I knew you had rights," she replied. "I just—"

"Ignored them?" he said, cutting her off. He paced around the table, despite the fact his legs had gone numb. "Played god. Did exactly what you wanted and to hell with the consequences? Was this the ultimate way for you to make me pay for my leaving town and joining the military?"

"No," she said quickly. "Everything I did, I did for T.J."

"T.J.?" He said his son's name and experienced an excruciating pain in the center of his chest. "Goddammit, Abby, you named him after Tom?"

She shook her head. "I named him after you," she refuted quickly. "T.J. stands for Tobias Jacob…your name flipped around."

Heat burned behind his eyes and he blinked, determined not to fall to pieces. He had to think, not react. Jake took a breath and met her gaze levelly. "Damn you, Abby. Damn you and your lying heart."

He had to get away. He needed time to digest it all. Jake strode from the room, not daring to look at her. He grabbed his things and was out of the house and back on his motorbike within minutes. He wasn't sure where he was going. But he had to clear his head. He had to make sense out of the chaos churning through his blood.

He drove around for a while and somehow ended up at his brother's house.

Joss met him on the porch, and they sat down on the steps, ignoring the cold morning air.

"You sure do look like crap," Joss said and bumped his shoulder affectionately. "I take it you had no idea?"

He frowned. "Nope. Did you?"

Joss shrugged. "I suspected."

So, Abby was right. "How? Why?"

His brother shrugged again. "I see Abby and the boy at the school sometimes. I never thought the kid looked anything like Tom Perkins. But he looks a hell of a lot like you."

"You've never said anything?"

Joss looked at him with obvious regret. "I should have, but I wasn't sure. And you…" His words trailed off.

"Are never around," he said, finishing the sentence.

Joss nodded. "We hardly talk. And I know that's just as much my issue and my fault as yours," he added, "but time passes and things remain unsaid."

Jake sighed, realizing his brother was right. And that T.J. *did* look like him, something he should have been smart enough to see weeks ago. He'd spent a lot of time with Abby and T.J. over the last couple of weeks but had been so blinded by his desire for Abby, anything else had taken a back seat. Sex had foolishly blinded his judgment. But not anymore. "I still can't believe she didn't tell me."

"I imagine she had her reasons," his brother said quietly. "You *had* left town again—maybe she thought you were never coming back."

"That's no excuse," he said coldly.

"No," Joss agreed. "But it might be a reason. The thing

is, having kids changes how a person views things. Look, I might talk a good line, but I would lay down my life for my girls in a heartbeat. And I would do anything to protect them. And maybe that's what Abby thought she was doing."

"By keeping him a secret? By lying by omission?" Jake shook his head irritably. "I had a right to know he existed."

"Of course you did, but I gather that you and Abby didn't exactly part on great terms after you hooked up again, right?"

He shrugged. "It was complicated. After Tom's funeral we were both looking for something, I guess, and it just…happened." He looked at his brother and saw the other man's brow rise questioningly. "I'm not proud of myself, okay? I know it was inappropriate." Joss snorted. "I know we shouldn't have done it. I know I acted like a total jerk, and if anything, I should have tried to stop it. But Abby and I…" His voice trailed off, and he sucked in a long breath. "Like I said…it's complicated."

"Then uncomplicate it and go and talk to her," Joss suggested. "You've got a kid…that means your life is about to change, and silence will only make things worse."

He knew his brother was right. Jake got to his feet and grabbed his cell, punching out a quick text message.

We need to talk. The hotel. Three o'clock.

Abby spent the hour after Jake had left at her grandmother's, pacing the floorboards, cursing her own foolishness, her emotions in turmoil. As expected, Patience was understanding, but also realistic.

"You must have expected he would be angry," her grandmother said when Abby had finally settled at the kitchen table, her hands pressed together in a tight knot, staring at the cell phone she'd placed on the table and knowing she should call Jake to see how he was. Because they absolutely needed to talk.

"Of course," she replied, shuddering out a breath. "And he has a right to feel that way."

"But?"

Abby shook her head, feeling the weight of her turmoil press down on her shoulders. "Being angry isn't going to change anything."

"That's easy for you to say, I imagine," her grandmother said softly. "Since you've had T.J. in your life for six years and Jake hasn't."

She sighed heavily. "There's a lot we need to discuss." Her cell pinged, and she quickly looked at the message, then met her grandmother's curious gaze. "He wants to talk. Can you watch T.J.?"

Patience nodded. "You know I'm here for you, Abby."

"I know, Gran," she said and blinked back the tears in her eyes. "I don't know how I would have coped these last six years without you."

"You're stronger that you realize," her grandmother said and patted her arm comfortingly. "And I know you'll get through this."

"I shouldn't have gotten so involved with him these past couple of weeks," she said frankly. "I mean, I wanted him to spend some time with T.J., but all I've done by giving in to my feelings for Jake is make things way more complicated."

Her grandmother knew Jake had spent the night, since his motorbike wasn't exactly subtle, and although she knew Patience wouldn't judge her decisions, she was always the voice of reason.

"Are you still in love with him?"

She shuddered out a breath. "Does it matter?"

"So, you're not?" Patience asked, digging deeper.

"I don't usually make rash decisions. You know how I've typically been so focused about everything I've wanted. I've been that way since I was young. Like how I knew since I was little that I wanted to be a chef. Or that I didn't want to be with someone in the military. Or how I wanted to study cooking in Paris. And then how I wanted to marry Tom and have a baby. I had all these great plans for my life, but all the while there was Jake Culhane in the background. The one part of myself I've never truly been able to control. Do I still love Jake?" She sighed and then shuddered. "I honestly don't want to think about what that would mean for me, Gran. Not when T.J. is going to be stuck in the middle."

"It's hard not to follow your heart, Abby," her grandmother said soothingly. "Believe me, I've done it myself in the past. But when it comes to Jake, I don't think you've ever really seen things clearly. I've always referred to him as your quicksand, because he's like something you might believe you can step across without being dragged down, but you really can't." She sighed gently. "I never truly approved of your relationship when you were young, Abby. I thought it was way too intense for you."

"You never liked him," she said.

"I didn't dislike him," Patience amended. "But it doesn't matter how I feel. It matters how *you* feel. Because now that he knows about T.J., things between you are going to be different. They'll have to be. That's probably something you should have foreseen before you invited him back into your bed."

"I know, Gran. It was a mistake."

She was still thinking about her grandmother's words as she headed for the hotel a little later. After the wedding, while she was hyped up on romance and memory and the feel of Jake's arms around her while they danced on the porch, and later, when they'd made love, she had convinced herself she was as much in love with him as always. But in the cold reality of day, things looked very different. The sex had turned her brain to mush. It had made her believe, for a few hours at least, that they had somehow found their way back to one another. And that it would work out. Perhaps if she'd taken the opportunity to tell Jake about T.J., then reconciliation would still seem possible. But the way he'd discovered the truth, with his brother as witness, now made that seem unlikely. And she knew she needed to think only of T.J. and what that truth meant for him.

When she reached the hotel, she texted Jake, and he asked her to meet him in his room. She didn't argue and quickly made her way upstairs, using her pass card for the elevator. His door was open when she arrived, and he stood aside as she crossed the threshold. He was in one of the larger suites, with a separate bedroom and living area and a view that overlooked the main road; the silhouette of the Black Hills could be seen in the distance. Abby dropped her tote, removed her coat and laid them both on the sofa, then sat down.

"Coffee?" he asked quietly.

She shook her head, thinking about how the black chambray shirt he wore stretched across his broad shoulders. Memories of the night before bombarded her. Of his kiss, his touch, his intimate possession, of every softly spoken word, and then of words unsaid.

"I'm sorry, Jake," she said quietly, meeting his gaze. "I know that's inadequate, considering the circumstances."

He moved around the sofa and sat down on a single chair, resting his elbows on his knees.

"It *is* inadequate. I want the truth," he said quietly. "Why didn't you tell me?"

"You left town and I—"

"I mean," he said and held up a hand, "why didn't you tell me last week, or last night?"

"I tried," she said softly. "I really did. But the time never seemed right. And I know that's no excuse," she added swiftly. "I know I've had plenty of opportunity to tell you these past couple of weeks. I think I wanted to see how T.J. responded to you and—"

"You were testing me?" he asked bluntly. "Seeing if I was good enough to be a father to him?"

It sounded bad. But it was exactly what she had done. She sighed. "Yes."

"Do you know how goddamned arrogant that sounds, Abby?"

She nodded. "I had to protect him."

"From me?" he asked incredulously.

"From disappointment," she replied. "From possible rejection. From the unknown."

He sighed wearily. "Do you truly believe I would do that? That I would knowingly *not* acknowledge my own son?"

She shrugged a little, knowing her response was inadequate. "I couldn't be sure."

"You know me better than that," he remarked coolly.

"I know you haven't been back to Cedar River in six years," she reminded him. "I know you've made it clear in the past that this town is not your home. I know you have a life in Sacramento and, for all I know, a woman who—"

"I'm single," he said and let out an impatient breath. "I've told you that already. And I certainly wouldn't have spent last night with you if I had some secret lover hidden away in Sacramento. I'm not a liar, Abby. You, on the other hand…"

Abby jumped to her feet. "Okay, you made your point. But I'm not going to apologize for wanting to protect my son."

"Our son," he corrected. "And I think that apologies are kind of useless at this point."

"Then what do you want?"

"For starters," he replied, "I'd like to know everything about him."

Abby walked toward the window, wrapped her arms around herself and replied. "He'll be six in March. He was four pounds, two ounces, when he was born—I already told you he was seven weeks early. He was in the hospital in Denver for five weeks, and I was with him every day. He had some breathing issues because his lungs weren't fully developed. But now he's perfectly healthy and, as you know, highly intelligent and academically advanced for his age."

"So, you left town after the funeral and returned with a baby that everyone assumed was conceived with your husband?"

She turned around, saw that Jake was still on the chair, his expression unwavering. "I never actually *said* he was Tom's."

"And didn't say he *wasn't*, right?"

Abby quickly grabbed her tote and rummaged through it, finding the envelope she'd placed in there that morning. She dropped the paper onto the coffee table in front of him.

"What's this?" he asked.

"Take a look."

Seconds later he had the envelope open and was reading the contents. "His birth certificate?"

"Your name is on that," she said quietly. "Not Tom's."

The paper shook in his hand, and he quickly met her gaze. "Well, that's something, at least."

"I know it looks as though I was keeping him a secret, and I know I should have told you about him sooner, but the truth is, no one has ever questioned whether he was Tom's child. I kept my married name after Tom's death, so that's why his surname is Perkins."

He dropped the certificate onto the table. "He needs to know the truth," Jake said flatly. "And that's not negotiable, Abby."

"Of course he needs to know," she said and sighed. "But *I* need to know what you want, or expect."

Jake got to his feet and faced her squarely. "I want," he said slowly, "the opportunity to get to know my son, and for him to get to know me. I expect," he added, "your full support."

There was no gentleness in his voice. No forgiveness. Nothing that made her think they could have a truce. They were on opposite ends. In a matter of hours, she had become his enemy.

"Of course. I'll tell him today."

"*We'll* tell him," he corrected. "And not today. I need some time to digest this, Abby. A couple of days. And I want to spend some time with him before we tell him. T.J. needs to know he can trust me before we make some big announcement. I don't want to upset or scare him."

"He already thinks you've hung the moon," she said quietly, pleased that Jake was thinking of T.J.'s welfare above anything else. "I know my son. I know he's going to welcome this news."

"You think?"

"Yes," she replied. "T.J. wants a father."

"He thinks Tom is his father," he reminded her.

"I know. But I've always refered to Tom as his angel daddy," she explained and inhaled deeply. "And as someone who watches over him and protects him. Because on some level, I always knew this day would come and wanted to make the transition as uncomplicated as possible."

Jake didn't look the least bit comforted by her assurances, and Abby couldn't blame him.

"Still, let's wait a couple of days," he insisted. "But I would like to see him tomorrow."

"Sure," she agreed. "After school?"

Jake nodded. "And then we'll need to agree to a schedule."

Abby suspected she'd have to be more flexible than she was used to. Jake had leverage, and she knew he would use it. "You can spend as much time with him as you would like before you leave."

His brows shot up. "Leave? Where precisely do you think I'm going?"

"Home," she replied. "Sacramento."

"I think we both know I'm not about to rush back to California."

She frowned a fraction. "But your business…your life?"

He made a scoffing sound. "What's this, Abby? Another one of your tests to see if I'll make the grade in the father department? To see how far I'll go to prove I can be an involved and responsible parent?"

"No," she muttered. "I only thought you'd need to go back."

"Unless you plan on packing his things and letting my son come with me, then no, I don't imagine I'll be returning to Sacramento in the foreseeable future."

So he was staying. Just like that.

"I didn't expect you would just drop your life and stay."

"Then what did you expect, Abby?" he shot back. "Oh, hang on, you didn't plan on telling me, so the point is moot, right?"

"I *was* going to tell you," she refuted. "I tried…last night I tried. But we were…things were…we…"

"You mean sex clouded the truth?" he asked bluntly. "You're right, it did. *It does.* Well, we won't have that problem anymore. The best thing for us both is for us to keep our hands off one another. That way our judgment won't get clouded again. And our son won't be stuck in the middle."

Abby wasn't about to disagree. Because sex *had* made things complicated. Wanting Jake and then giving in to that desire had impaired her judgment and added another layer of complication to an already difficult situation.

And what did he mean by the "forseeable future"? She longed to ask him how long he was planning to stick around, but she knew she wasn't in a position to make demands. Later, once the dust had settled, once T.J. knew the whole truth, then she would ask him for details.

"Well, I guess I should go," she said quietly and grabbed her tote and coat. "For what it's worth, I never deliberately set out to deny you the opportunity to be his father. I know," she said and held up a hand, "that it looks that way. But I always believed you didn't want to be in Cedar River, and as time passed the idea of contacting you just got too hard. I guess that makes me a coward as well as a liar. See you tomorrow."

She left the suite without another word and hardly took a breath as she scurried down the corridor and entered the elevator. Once she was outside and back in her car, Abby burst into tears, crying for all she'd done, and all she'd lost. Including the trust of the first man she'd ever loved…and the father of her child.

As promised, Jake came to see T.J. the following afternoon. Abby had called in sick that day, too weary and upset to drag herself out of the house and face the world. She'd barely slept and knew she looked ghastly pale and tired when he arrived at five o'clock, holding up a couple of bags of takeout from JoJo's. He'd texted earlier and said he was bringing dinner, and she didn't have the strength to argue *or* comply. As he had requested, her grandmother was in attendance. Abby had no idea why he wanted Patience to be there, but she figured she wasn't in a position to be disagreeable and if her grandmother was surprised by his request, she didn't say anything.

"It's good to see you again, Jake," her grandmother said politely.

"Likewise," he said and passed Abby the food bags. "Where's T.J.?"

"Just finishing his reading homework. I told him you were dropping by, and he's very happy. I didn't say anything," she amended when she saw his expression narrow. "As you wanted. His room is the second on the right, just down the hall off the living room if you—"

"Actually," he said quietly, cutting her off, "I'd like to speak with your grandmother…alone."

Abby glanced toward Patience and nodded. "I'll go and see if he's done with his homework."

She left the room and could barely make out their quiet voices as she walked down the hall. Of course, she knew her grandmother was her ally and greatest supporter. But she also knew that Patience had spent a long time telling her that Jake had a right to know about his son. And of course, she was right. The mess she was in was all of her own doing.

"Mommy!" T.J. exclaimed when he spotted her standing in the doorway of his bedroom. "Is Jake here?"

She nodded and walked into the room. "He certainly is."

"Yay," he said excitedly and closed his book, quickly coming toward her. "I really like Jake, Mommy."

Abby's heart clenched, and she marveled at how attached her son had become to his father, without knowing he *was* his father. Perhaps it was simple DNA, a connection that went beyond acquaintance and familiarity. Maybe nature overrode nurture. Or perhaps it was simply that T.J. longed so desperately for a father that he was instantly clinging to the first man who made the grade.

"I know you do, honey," she said gently and ruffled his hair. "And I'm sure you'll get to spend lots of time with him."

T.J. regarded her seriously. "Is he…"

Abby's breath stuck in her throat. Her son was smart. Perhaps he'd worked it out. "Is he what, honey?"

T.J. shrugged. "Is he gonna take me snowboarding again?"

"I think so," she said and sighed softly with relief.

When she returned to the kitchen with T.J. in tow, Jake and her grandmother were conspicuously absent. Her son sulked for a moment, until he spotted the takeout bags from JoJo's on the countertop and then spent several minutes trying to guess what was inside.

It was another ten minutes before Jake and Patience returned through the back door. They were both laughing, and T.J. raced toward Jake and high-fived him, jumping around excitedly.

"Everything okay?" Abby asked, curious and concerned.

Patience nodded. "Of course. I've just agreed to lease the apartment above the garage to Jake for a few weeks."

She stilled instantly. "Huh?"

"What your grandmother means," Jake said quietly, "is that I'll be living next door."

Abby waited for her heart to beat, waited for her breath to push from her lungs, waited for the freight train racing through her blood to come to a halt. Next door? So close he would almost be in arm's reach.

But so far away…because she knew his arms would never be around her again.

Chapter Nine

Jake couldn't believe how nervous he was about the prospect of telling a nearly six-year-old boy that he was his father. He'd had twenty-four hours to get used to the idea, but the truth was, he was terrified.

Moving into Patience's apartment had been a spur-of-the-moment decision and one he knew would be the best thing for his son—even though the thought of being so close to Abby twenty-four-seven made him uneasy. But hearing T.J.'s delighted and animated reaction when he was told he would be living next door, more than compensated for any reluctance he was feeling.

"Mommy," T.J. said as he pulled himself onto a counter stool in the kitchen. "Can Jake have dinner with us every night from now on?"

Abby met Jake's gaze and then looked at their son. "We'll see, okay?"

T.J. rattled the bags of takeout Jake had brought with him. "Now that everybody's here, can we eat?"

Abby nodded, grabbed plates and quickly moved the food and dinnerware to the table. Jake listened as T.J. chatted through dinner, hearing stories about the upcoming concert at school, about when he wanted to have another snowboarding lesson, and how they could hang out all the time now that he would be living next door.

"So, Jake," Patience Reed said once T.J. had left the

kitchen to get his reading homework done. "Abby tells me you have a successful business back in Sacramento?"

"Yes," he replied and explained briefly what he did. "I got a degree in software engineering while I was in the army and when I retired it kind of all came together. I was lucky to find a good business partner."

"Yes," the older woman said as Abby collected the plates. "A good partner is important in all aspects of life."

He got her point, and wanted to tell her she was way off base. "Mrs. Reed, I—"

"Patience," she corrected. "It's probably time you called me that, don't you think?"

"I guess so."

"Gran," Abby said, glancing toward the doorway. "Please don't—"

"I'll say this now, and not mention it again," Patience said quietly. "You both need to get over this tension that's between you. Because that little boy is smart and he'll figure things out quickly. I know you're angry," she said and gestured toward Jake. "And you have reason to be. But," she added and offered a supportive smile, "my great-grandson's happiness is what matters most. And for him to be happy, the pair of you need to get along. Fake it if you have to," she said and got to her feet. "But do it."

Once she left and headed out the rear door, Jake stood up and moved toward the countertop. "She's right."

Abby stopped rattling dishes and looked at him. "Of course she's right. That doesn't make it any easier."

"I guess not. Can I see him tomorrow?"

She nodded. "Of course. Same time. Only I'll cook."

Jake managed a tense smile. "I'll just drop by his room and say good-night. See you tomorrow."

Once he'd said good-night to T.J., Jake left Abby's house and headed back to the hotel. He had a restless night, but looked forward to seeing his son. He didn't stay for dinner again the following evening, but did hang out with T.J. for an hour. As always, T.J. was happy to see him, and he wondered if his son suspected that Jake was more than a simple friend. And more than anything, he hoped T.J. would be happy with the news that he was his dad.

On Thursday Jake moved into the apartment above Patience's garage. It was a big space, with one large bedroom, a kitchen, combined living and dining room and a small bathroom. The place was newly renovated and more than adequate for his needs. The laundry was downstairs, which he didn't mind, and Patience had agreed he could park his bike in the garage. The most important thing was that it was so close to his son.

His son...

Just thinking about it made him both ache inside and feel anxious. Particularly since he and Abby had agreed they would tell him on Thursday. Jake had arranged for his personal assistant, Roberta, a woman in her late-forties who'd been working for the company since he and Trent had started the business, to pack some of his belongings at his apartment and send them to Cedar River. He was making his latest trip up the stairs at the side of the garage with yet another box when his cell rang. Spotting Trent's number on the screen, he answered.

"Did you get your stuff?" Trent asked.

"Yes, say thank you again to Roberta."

"How long are you staying?" his friend queried.

"Indefinitely at this stage."

His friend and partner knew the whole story, from his brother's accident and why he'd returned in the first place, to why he was now staying, and in the past couple of days they had discussed ways for them to still run the business from a distance. They were both prepared to give it a shot for the moment, trying out the arrangement for a few months, and considering how easily he'd facilitated the contract for the O'Sullivan Hotel, neither imagined they'd run into any problems. The main thing was, Jake was planning on staying in Cedar River. At this stage, permanently.

His family had taken the news about T.J.'s paternity with a varying degree of responses. Mitch was naturally annoyed by Abby's deception and cautioned Jake to take things slowly, but mostly they were all delighted by the idea of having a nephew to dote on. He discovered that Ellie wasn't all that surprised and muttered something about them having the same name, something she'd discreetly questioned T.J. about during the sleepover after the wedding.

"Good luck," Trent said.

"Yeah," Jake said and chuckled wryly. "I'm gonna need it."

Jake ended the call and spotted Abby and T.J. at the bottom of the stairs. She wore jeans and high boots, a bright purple sweater, and a white wool jacket with matching beanie and scarf and looked so damned beautiful the air rushed through his lungs like wind. And then he cursed himself for being so predictable. He'd been fighting his attraction for her all week, using his resentment to fuel his anger, but keeping his feelings in check so that T.J. wouldn't pick up on any tension between them. The last thing he wanted was for his son to suspect they were in the middle of a silent war. Because that's what it felt like. And crazily, it was rougher than any real war zone he'd been in. He *wanted* to hate her so much he could taste it. But he couldn't. And that was the damnable misery of it.

Which helped with his resentment, of course, and amplified the self-loathing he was experiencing. The truth was, they'd barely spoken two words all week. She'd tried a few times while he'd been visiting with T.J., but Jake was so freaking mad he barely responded, figuring that at this stage silence was better than all-out confrontation. Or maybe they needed an argument to help him get the frustration out of his system. And sure, Patience's warning was never far from his thoughts. He knew he had to get his act together—but he was so damned hurt by Abby's betrayal, he could barely think straight.

"I need to go into town for a few things," she said, looking up at him. "Can you watch T.J.?"

Jake nodded. "Of course."

His son quickly raced up the stairs, and Jake experienced an unfamiliar sensation in the center of his chest. Joy, he thought absently. Knowing how much T.J. was pleased by the idea of spending time with him.

They'd been moving and unpacking boxes for about twenty minutes, with T.J. chatting on about school and how he was looking forward to snowboarding again that weekend. There was something infectious about his little-boy laugh, and Jake couldn't help but marvel at how incredible he was. He was smart and had a natural curiosity about things and was always asking questions.

"Jake?"

Jake was under the desk in the corner of the living room, plugging in the small printer to finish off the nook as his office, when he spotted T.J. standing at his side. "Yes, buddy," he said and continued with the task.

"Are you my daddy?"

Jake jerked and hit his head on the underside of the desk, cursing silently as he quickly shifted position and sat up. T.J. was regarding him thoughtfully, his head to one side, biting his lower lip exactly as his mother often did.

"Ah…what makes you think that?" he asked, barely able to breath.

T.J. met his gaze. "Because Mommy said I looked like my daddy. But my angel daddy had red hair and freckles and I don't. I have brown hair and no freckles," he said and reached out, threading his small fingers through Jake's hair for a moment. "Like you."

Jake took a breath, considered the importance of the moment and knew he wasn't in a position to lie or make excuses or be evasive. In a perfect situation, he and Abby should have been telling him together. But it wasn't a perfect situation. And his son—this beautiful child who needed him to be worthy of being his father—deserved the truth.

"Yes," he said quietly, grasping T.J.'s hand. "I am."

T.J.'s eyes widened. "Like…you're really my daddy?"

Jake nodded again. "That's right. Is that okay?"

Jake watched, fascinated as his son considered the news, anticipating more questions, more query and explanation. But T.J. only smiled and then unexpectedly threw himself against Jake, wrapping small arms around his neck. As the shock subsided, Jake experienced something…a feeling completely new to him, one that threatened to rock him to the soles of his feet and the core of his very being. His chest tightened, and suddenly it was impossible to breathe. His eyes burned, his ribs hurt and everything he'd imagined he would feel spectacularly disappeared, and he experienced an acute and intense surge of love and affection for the little boy who was clinging so joyously to him. He blinked away the heat in his eyes and hugged him back, all his fear disappearing, because T.J. made it so easy.

"I'm so lucky," T.J. said happily. "I have an angel daddy and you, Jake."

Jake swallowed hard, fighting back emotion. "You certainly do."

They talked for a while, with his son bouncing out questions about all the things they could do, all the places they could go. T.J. didn't ask any difficult questions, about Tom, or his mom, or about why Jake hadn't been around, but he suspected they would come. When Abby returned about an hour later, the first thing T.J. did was race to the door to greet her and make the big announcement.

"Mommy, Mommy, Jake's my daddy!"

Jake was by the door in a few seconds and caught her frown. "How about you let Mommy come inside out of the cold."

He stood aside and let his mother pass, then gave them a quizzical look. "I'm gonna go and tell Great-Gran. Is that okay, Mommy?"

He saw Abby nod vaguely, and once T.J. was down the stairs, Jake spoke. "Before you react and start blaming me for overstepping, I didn't tell *him*, he asked *me*."

She sighed and wrapped her arms around herself. "Well, like Gran said, he's smart, so it's not entirely unexpected. He's been asking a lot of questions the last couple of weeks. About having a father. About Tom. About you. He's never had a man in his sphere other than his teachers and soccer coach. I guess he just connected all the dots and figured it out. Did he ask you why—"

"Why I've been missing from his life for the past six years?" Jake said, cutting her off, trying to push back his frustration, and failing. "Not yet, but I don't doubt those questions will come at some point. I'm sure he'll have some for you, too."

She nodded, her eyes so bright he could have sworn

they glistened with tears and then hated how that made him feel. He didn't want to feel empathy toward Abby. He didn't want to feel anything. It was too hard. He wanted to stay mad—to compartmentalize his feelings. That way, he didn't have to revisit how he *really* felt about Abby.

"He looked so happy. I'm really pleased that he's become attached to you, Jake. He's been wanting this for such a long time."

She was being completely reasonable, and it irritated him to no end. "Better late than never, right?"

Her eyes flashed for a microsecond, but then reasonable, accommodating Abby was back. "I need to go into Rapid City on Saturday to do some Christmas shopping, so if you want to have T.J. for the day, you can. I think he's looking forward to another snowboarding lesson."

He nodded. "Sure."

She half smiled and looked around. "It's nice in here. Gran had it renovated earlier this year. It was a sensible idea for you to move in."

He laughed humorlessly. "Give me a break, Abby. I know you'd prefer me to stay at the hotel or, I suspect, go back to Sacramento."

"That's not true," she refuted hotly.

"Isn't it?" he queried. "Wouldn't you like your life to return to the secretive and uncomplicated one you had before I came back to town?"

She plonked her hands on her hips. "I want him to have a relationship with you, Jake. He's the most important thing in the world to me, and his happiness is my priority. Perhaps my past actions haven't made that apparent, but I'm trying to make amends to T.J....and to you."

Jake waved an impatient hand. "Okay, you've made your point. You'll be as obliging as possible to make up for denying me the right to know my son for the past six years."

Her eyes brightened instantly, and she swallowed hard. "You're looking for an argument, but I'm not going to give you one."

He knew she was right to say it and also knew that Abby could read his moods. Despite the years they'd been apart, their connection was still strong.

"I'm trying, Abby," he admitted and exhaled. "But this situation is hard to make right in my mind. And for the record, I didn't plan on telling T.J. I was his father without you being here. It just sort of happened. He asked me and I…" His words trailed off for a moment, and then he quickly refocused. "I owed him the truth." She nodded. "I understand. Sometimes parenting is about improvising. I do it all the time. I'll see you later."

She left the apartment, and once she was down the stairs, Jake expelled a long breath. He was right about his motives—imagining that arguing with her was at least better than the neutrality he'd struggled to endure over the last few days. And not that he had any intention of arguing with Abby in front of their son…but he was struggling with his anger and resentment and was desperately trying to figure out what he was feeling.

And obviously failing.

When T.J. returned to his apartment, he was carrying his electronic tablet and insisted on playing a game with Jake before dinner. They hung out together for a while, then at five thirty, he walked T.J. home. Abby was in the kitchen, steaming jars he suspected were for the holiday jelly his son had said she made every Christmas. She looked up and offered a tight smile, telling T.J. to get washed up for dinner. Once their son left the room, she spoke again.

"What are your holiday plans?"

Jake rested his hands on the countertop. "There'll be a shindig of some sort at the ranch. And I would like to spend some time with T.J. while he's off from school. You?"

"If I'm not working, Gran and I usually go to Florida to spend it with my mom."

Jake's insides twitched. "You do?"

She nodded. "Yes."

"And this year?"

She shrugged a little and waved a hand. "Well, of course I won't be going this year, as I'm sure T.J. will want to spend some time with you."

"I appreciate that."

God, they were so sweetly polite to one other at times it made his teeth ache.

"Would you like to stay for dinner?"

Jake's auto response was to refuse, but the idea of spending more time with T.J. appealed to him. And he *was* hungry. And he did like Abby's cooking.

And as much as he hated to admit it, he was getting tired of being alone with his thoughts and resentment.

He nodded. "Thank you. Can I help?"

She pushed the breadboard, sourdough loaf and knife across the counter. "You can cut."

He did the task quickly and tried not to look at her. Tried not to think about how the scent of her perfume or the way her hair flicked over her shoulders when she moved. When T.J. returned to the kitchen it got a little easier, and he was able to concentrate on their son, helping him toss the salad his mother had made.

"When I grow up I'm gonna be a chef like like mommy," T.J. said as Jake passed him a wedge of tomato. "Or a soldier, like my daddy."

Jake caught Abby's startled expression. Because he knew, without a doubt, that the last thing Abby would want is for T.J. to have a military career.

"You know," Jake said and gently smoothed a hand over his son's head. "I'm not a soldier any more. Now I work with computers. You like computers, right?"

T.J.'s interest was quickly diverted and he began chatting about his gaming console. Jake met Abby's gaze, saw relief and a hint of gratitude in her expression, which helped alleviate the tension between them.

Once dinner was over and T.J. was bathed and wearing his pajamas, he insisted Jake tuck him in for the night. He sat on the edge of the bed, reading from his son's favorite dinosaur book, and admired how Abby had decorated the room so lovingly. With the mobiles hanging from the ceiling and the duvet with cars printed on it, it was very much a place for a child to feel loved and safe.

"Jake?" T.J. said once the story was finished and he was tucked warmly beneath the covers.

"Yes?"

His son bit his lower lip for moment, then spoke. "Can I call you Daddy now?"

Jake's throat tightened with emotion, and his eyes burned. "Of course you can."

T.J. nodded, then smiled sleepily and closed his eyes. "Good night, Daddy."

"'Night, buddy."

When Jake returned to the kitchen, Abby was at the table folding laundry. He watched her for a moment, noticing the tiny furrow between her brows as she concentrated on the task, and then wondered why he couldn't control the crazy way his heart hammered behind his ribs when she was near. The physical connection between them defied his determination to stop thinking about her as anything other than the mother of his son. He didn't *want* to want her. In fact, he'd spent the past few days foolishly talking himself into loathing her...or at least trying to.

"Abby?"

She looked up and met his gaze. "Is he asleep?"

Jake nodded and took a breath. "I want..." He stopped, reevaluating his words. "I'd *like* for T.J. to have my last name. Is that something you would consider?"

"Of course," she said and nodded.

Her quick compliance surprised him. "Just like that?"

"Well, I suppose we should have some kind of transition period," she replied. "I've expected it. And I think T.J. will want it."

"You know people will talk?"

She nodded. "People *always* talk. I'm not blind to what it will mean for him. For us, too. Change, certainly. And probably idle gossip. But also the chance to be a part of your family. Your brothers and sister are good people, Jake, I have no hesitation in wanting T.J. to be a part of that. Your family has lived in this town for generations, and they are an important part of Cedar River's history. I want my son to know that he's a part of that legacy."

It sounded too good to be true. Abby was saying exactly what he wanted to hear. And they both knew it. It couldn't last, he was sure. At some point, Abby was going to object to one of his demands and set boundaries.

"We need to set up a parenting schedule," he said quietly.

Her eyes narrowed. "Ah...okay. Although you can see T.J. anytime you want to."

"I was thinking of something a little more formal," he said and rested one shoulder against the doorjamb.

"Formal," she echoed and stopped folding clothes. "You mean like a custody arrangement?"

"Exactly."

She was silent for a moment and pressed a hand down on the pile of clothes. "I'm not sure I see why that's necessary."

"Necessary?" he queried and pushed himself off the door. "You kept my son a secret for six years, Abby, so I'm not sure I can trust you not to disappear into the night with him for another six years."

Abby had been expecting the hard conversations. And even this one, she supposed. Jake had the right to question her intentions, but it hurt that he still didn't trust her and saddened her to think they had such a huge divide between them.

"This town is my home," she assured him tightly. "And T.J.'s home. This is where he feels safe and loved. If I wanted to hide him from the world, I would have stayed in Denver and raised him there. But I didn't. I came back to Cedar River because I love this town."

"Nice speech," he shot back. "But Abby, you've already lied to me for six years, so I'm not sure what to believe."

Her hurt returned. A bone-deep, heart-wrenching hurt that had been consuming her for days. Of course, she knew Jake had every right to question her motives, and to be angry. But it still made her ache inside knowing he thought so badly of her.

"You can believe me now, Jake," she assured him.

"I want to," he said and sighed heavily. "For our son's sake."

The mood between them didn't shift for the following couple of days, but they did manage to settle into a routine of sorts. On Saturday, Abby headed into Rapid City to do some Christmas shopping with Patience and Annie, and T.J. stayed at home with his father. Hanging out with

Jake, it seemed, had become her son's favorite thing to do in the whole world. To say her friend was shocked to discover the truth of T.J.'s paternity was an understatement. Patience headed off to the local department store, leaving Abby and Annie to take a break at a nearby café.

"So, what about you and Jake?" Annie asked over cake and coffee.

"There is no me and Jake," she said flatly.

"But I thought, after the wedding, you know…you guys…"

"It was just sex," she admitted and ached all over thinking about it.

"To him?" Annie said and raised a brow. "Or to you?"

"I'm not going to waste time imagining that Jake and I are going to have some romantic happily-ever-after," she said and sighed. "He's T.J.'s father, and that's all. Besides, he's made it very clear what he thinks of me for not telling him about T.J."

"He has a point, though," Annie said frankly. "I mean, you did keep it a secret."

"No one ever asked," she said. "People assumed he was Tom's and I—"

"I get it, Abby," Annie said gently. "You felt like you were backed into a corner and couldn't explain. It's not so hard to understand."

"It is for Jake," she remarked and sipped her coffee.

"He's reacting because he's in the middle of something that's completely out of his control. Give him time. I'm sure he'll come around and understand your reasons."

Abby wasn't so sure. The past couple of days had been difficult ones. Of course, T.J. was happier than she had ever seen him, and Abby was delighted her son had a father to call his own. When Jake wasn't around, T.J. talked about him constantly. And Tom, too. Abby answered as truthfully as she could, gently explaining the difference between his *angel daddy* and his *real daddy* and he seemed to accept her explanation. However, witnessing the affection growing between them only amplified the guilt she felt knowing she was responsible for keeping them apart for so long. And guilt was a harsh companion. It weakened her defenses against her feelings for Jake and made loving him acutely painful. Of course, he could never know she still loved him. That would only add humiliation to her already fragile emotions.

By the time she pulled into the driveway that afternoon, it was past two o'clock. She left her packages in the car, since she knew T.J. would begin questioning who they were for the moment she got them into the house. Although he was an incredibly curious and smart child, he still believed in the magic of Christmas and Santa Claus, and she wanted him to hold on to those beliefs as long as he could. She heard the television as soon she opened the front door, but she was drawn to the sound of voices coming from the kitchen. She was down the hall and about to turn the corner when T.J.'s voice stopped her in her tracks.

"Daddy, why didn't you come back and be my daddy a long time ago?"

There was a long silence, and she remained behind the kitchen doorway, conscious that she was in the middle of a private conversation between father and son. Of course, she knew T.J. would ask difficult questions. But she didn't know how Jake would answer them.

"Because I didn't know about you," Jake replied quietly.

"But why?"

Because your mom never told me you existed...

"Because I had to go away, and no one knew where I was," he said, and she heard the clink of cutlery. "I was a soldier, very far away. Remember how we talked about that the other day? And I was a long way from here."

"Why didn't Mommy call you? Don't soldiers have phones, Daddy?"

Jake cleared his throat a little. "Of course," he replied. "But your mommy didn't have my phone number."

Relief pitched in her chest. And something else. Gratitude. It would be easy for Jake to make her out as the bad guy, to blame her, to give her the responsibility of explaining the real truth to their son.

"But Mommy could have tried, couldn't she?" T.J. asked relentlessly.

"No, she couldn't," Jake said quietly. "Mommy had to spend all her time looking after you, because you're the most important person in the world to her."

T.J. took a few seconds, then spoke again. "I wish Mommy had your phone number, Daddy, because then you would have known I was here the whole time."

"Well, I'm here now, buddy."

"Forever?"

"Yes," Jake said, and Abby swallowed the lump burning in her throat. "I'm not going anywhere."

"I'm glad. You know, once Mommy couldn't find a phone number and she looked in the big book that Great-Gran has, the one with all the numbers in it."

The simplicity of T.J.'s reasoning was impossible to ignore, and an all-too-familiar guilt pressed down on Abby's shoulders. She took a breath, waiting for Jake's response, feeling like an intruder as she listened on the sidelines but was unable to drag herself away.

"If Mommy had any way of telling me, she would have," Jake assured their son. "But it's not Mommy's fault, okay? It's all my fault I didn't come back sooner. Can you forgive me?"

Abby's throat burned, and she pressed back against the wall, breathing heavily. She gathered her composure and walked back down the hall, opening the front door loudly. She heard footsteps racing from the kitchen, and T.J. was quickly in front of her.

"Mommy! Mommy! Daddy and me had the best time ever today!"

Abby hugged him close, looking up briefly to see Jake standing in the hallway. "You did? That's wonderful. Do you think you could go and read in your room for a while so that I can talk to your dad about a few things?"

Her son looked reflective for a moment, then nodded. "Sure, Mommy. Are you looking for a place to hide my Christmas presents?"

She grinned. "Nope, they're already hidden. Only Santa knows where they are."

"Not Daddy?" he asked and frowned.

"Well, yes, Daddy too," she corrected, knowing how important it was for Jake to be included within the frame of their son's reasoning.

Once he was out of sight, Abby looked back toward Jake. "Can we go into the living room to talk?"

He nodded and followed her into the front room, waiting while she half closed the door. "What did you want to talk about?" he asked.

"About T.J. He's so happy at the moment. Thank you, Jake," she said and swallowed the lump of emotion in her throat. "For being everything that he'd hoped for."

Jake's eyes glittered brilliantly. "He's a wonderful child, Abby. You've done an amazing job raising him alone."

"I had help," she admitted and shrugged. "Gran was always here to help me, and I've had great friends, too. But I appreciate your confidence in my parenting, although it hasn't always been easy." She hesitated. "There's a Christmas concert at his school next week, and there's also a teacher/parent meeting coming up in a few weeks. I'll let you know the date so you can be there if you want to."

"Yes, I would," he said quietly. "I'd really love to be there for both. It's obvious that he's smart and that he requires more academic stimulation than most six-year-olds."

"He does," she agreed and drew in a breath. "And thank you for what you said."

"What I said? About what?"

"I mean, what you *didn't* say," she corrected. "I heard you earlier, when T.J. was asking why you haven't been in his life. I know you could have said something very different. I appreciate how you—"

"Anything I said," he said quietly, "I said for my son's sake. He doesn't need to know the details. And he certainly doesn't need to think badly of his mother. I'm not that petty, Abby. The fact is, I'm very proud to be his father and plan to do a much better job than my own ever did."

"I know you will."

He stared at her, going deep into her eyes, into that place she'd always saved for only him. She saw so much in his gaze—anger, resentment, bitterness, betrayal, disbelief—so many emotions she knew he had every right to feel. But it still hurt. And she saw something else, too. The awareness that still throbbed between them. It would never wane, she was certain. It had been set ablaze when they were sixteen, and nothing would dilute their attraction for one another.

Finally he spoke again. "Why did you do it?"

Abby twisted her hands tightly together. "I told you

why. I was confused and didn't know how to find you and—"

"Not that," he rasped, waving an impatient hand. "Why did you marry Tom? Why the hell did you marry my best friend?"

Abby gasped, and the real truth teetered on the edge of her tongue. "Because I… I wanted to…"

"You wanted to what?" he demanded.

Abby swallowed hard and shuddered. "I wanted to punish you for leaving me."

His gaze narrowed, and he made a scoffing sound. "Well, you certainly realized your ambition."

"I was so young, and I blamed you for not staying."

"I told you why I had to leave," he shot back. "I didn't want to end up like my father."

"You wouldn't have," she said quickly.

"You sure about that?" he queried. "I was angry and hotheaded back then. I hated my old man and everything he stood for. I had the devil on my back, Abby, and I knew the only way to ditch that devil was to live a life that was structured and disciplined. I knew the military would channel all that rage into something else. Because of what happened to your dad, I thought you'd understand."

"*Because* of my dad," she entreated, "I didn't understand at all. I knew the risks, Jake, better than anyone. What if something had happened to you? What if you were injured, or worse? I knew I didn't have the strength for any more loss. I didn't want to be a soldier's wife. A soldier's *widow*. I didn't want my children to be without a father."

"And yet, ironically," he said, his mouth tightening, "our son has been without his father for nearly the first six years of his life. Don't you think the odds would have been better if you stuck with us back when we were young?"

"Maybe," she admitted. "But I wanted—"

"To punish me?" he repeated her words as though they injured him to his very core.

"I'm not proud of my behavior."

"I hear you, Abby. I'm smart enough to figure out that I'm not exactly blameless in this…but I still have a hard time understanding. The truth is, at the time I was sure that you'd find a way to be okay with me enlisting and then we'd get back together. But no…you took off to Paris with Tom."

"You told Tom you were okay with us getting married."

"What the hell did you expect me to say?" he demanded, running a hand over his face. "I was being deployed, and two days before, I get a call from Tom asking me be the best man at his wedding to my *ex-girlfriend*. Of course I wasn't okay with it," he said, clearly frustrated. "I'm still not okay with you ditching me and then jumping into Tom's bed while I was at boot camp. I'm not okay with you marrying my best friend. And I'm not okay with you keeping my son's existence a secret for the last six years!"

He took a long breath, dragging air into his lungs, glaring at her. It was the first time he'd mentioned his feelings about her marrying Tom. Back then, she'd simply accepted his response as a man who no longer cared. But had she been wrong? She'd convinced herself he'd fallen out of love with her, choosing the military over their relationship, over *her*. It never occurred to her that he had still cared. If he had, he would have fought harder. And he wouldn't have enlisted in the first place.

"I didn't think you cared," she admitted hollowly.

He stared at her. "Seriously? Back in high school, we were as close as two people could be. When Hank had his accident, and when Billie-Jack left town and everything was turning to crap and family services was threatening to tear my family apart, *you* are what kept me sane. You kept me from allowing my hatred for Billie-Jack to consume me. You made it bearable. You were unfailingly supportive and always there when I needed you. And then you weren't," he added humorlessly. "And somehow, you ended up falling for my best friend and then marrying him."

"I thought we were over…"

"Over?" he laughed. "We have a child down the hall. We'll never be over, Abby."

They were close, barely a foot apart, and she felt the intensity of his frustration vibrating through her. Instinct made her reach out and rest a palm against his chest. His heart thundered beneath his rib cage, and she sucked in some air, trying to calm herself, trying to ease the turmoil racing through them both. And then, without another word, she was against him and his arms moved around her waist.

"I shouldn't have married Tom," she whispered, reaching up to touch his face.

His eyes bored into hers. "No, you shouldn't have."

He kissed her hotly, like they'd been starved of one another for an age. Abby pressed against him, running her hands up his strong back, feeling his muscles bunch, drawing the tension in his body deep into her fingertips. His tongue was in her mouth and she took it eagerly, feeling desire wind through her blood, knowing it was madness, knowing they both were kissing against their will. But the feelings between them were stronger than the resistance, more powerful than any bitterness or recrimination.

He finally pulled back, breaking the kiss, breathing

hard, his gaze boring into her, but he still held her in his arms. "I have to… I *need* to stop wanting you."

Why?

The word stayed on the edge of her tongue, but she longed to ask it, even though she knew the answer. *T.J.* Their attraction for one another was muddying the waters, and she knew Jake didn't want to be derailed in his determination to be a good father to their son.

"Then stop," she said quietly and pulled away, putting space between them, knowing she was as caught up in desire and attraction as he was.

Quicksand…

Gran was right. Jake would always be the one man she couldn't resist.

And the only man she would ever love.

Chapter Ten

"So, how are things going?"

Jake was at the Triple C late on Monday afternoon, hanging out with Mitch, Tess and Hank after spending a couple of hours in the saddle, helping out with mustering. He was also trying to ignore the constant pounding of the headache from hell that had been his companion for two long days.

He looked at his brother Mitch and shrugged. "Good."

"Are you enjoying being a dad?" Tess asked, her hand rested on her belly. His sister-in-law was only a few weeks away from having her baby and looked radiant about the prospect.

Jake nodded. "Very much."

"He's a lovely child, Jake," Tess said and smiled.

"I know," he said, pride filling his chest.

"And Abby?" Tess inquired.

Jake didn't wasn't to get into a discussion about his son's mother. The less he talked about Abby, the better. "It's complicated."

"That's what he says when he doesn't want to talk about it." It was Joss, standing in the doorway, holding an armload of wrapped gifts, who spoke. His brother strode into the room and dumped the presents by the tree. "A couple more loads and I should be done. If anyone wants to help, feel free to volunteer."

Mitch tapped the cast on his leg. "Count me out."

The whole family was planning on staying at the ranch over Christmas, including Grant, plus Joss and his girls. Jake knew it was Tess's idea—a way of bringing the family together over the holidays. He didn't mind, and intended spending some of the day with T.J. at the ranch if he could work out a schedule with Abby.

"I've got blisters from wrapping so many gifts," Joss said and grimaced.

Hank got to his feet. "Jesus, you whine like a little kid. Let's get these gifts inside."

The twins disappeared, and Jake was forced to face the inquisition of his eldest brother.

"You look like you need to talk," Mitch remarked.

"I'm all talked out," he said and sipped his coffee.

"Annie told me that Abby is really trying to make amends," Tess offered quietly.

"Amends?" Jake queried. "I don't see how she can. She lied to me for six years…that's not something that can be fixed in a week."

"You *could* forgive her," Mitch suggested. "I mean, I know we were surprised when you told us about T.J., but the most important thing in life is family—and Abby is T.J.'s mom and that makes her—"

"I know what she is," he said quickly. He *could* forgive her. If he wanted to get his heart smashed all over again. "I'm only interested in being T.J.'s father."

"That's why you look like you haven't slept for a week."

"Is there a point to this conversation?" he said irritably.

Mitch sighed. "The point is, we're worried about you."

"Don't be," Jake said and placed the mug on the side table. "I'm fine."

"You're not fine," Hank said as he walked back into the room with his big arms loaded with gifts, Joss a couple of steps behind him. "We can all see that."

Jake ignored the way his insides twitched. He cared about his family, but he didn't care for their intrusion into his thoughts and feelings. He wanted to be left alone, to work out his lingering resentment on his own. That was his way. How he'd always done things.

"Look, I appreciate everyone's *interest* in my well-being, but I really am doing okay. Finding out about T.J. was a shock, but I've accepted it and am happy knowing he's my son." He made an impatient gesture. "Now, can we talk about something else?"

"No," Joss replied and added more gifts underneath the tree. "This is a big deal. And despite how much we *all* know you hate talking about anything even remotely personal, you gotta face how you're feeling about this."

"Why?"

Joss shook his head. "Man, you're such a hard-ass. Is that what war did to you?"

"Look, just because I don't express every feeling I have every time I have them, doesn't mean I don't *feel*. I do, okay. But I'm not about to change who I am."

"You are changed," Joss said gently. "You're a father now…that's about as big a change as it gets."

Jake's head pounded. He didn't want to talk about what he was feeling. Hell, he didn't want to *think* about how he was feeling. But his family was relentless. And they didn't get it. They were a tight unit, and in a way, he'd always experienced an element of exclusion around them. He knew it wasn't deliberate, and he knew it was of his own making. He'd left. He was the one who'd wanted a different life and a way out to exorcise his demons and fears. He was the one who'd left town and had rarely shown his face in fourteen years.

He jumped to his feet impatiently. "What the hell do you want me to say? That I'm pissed? That I'm so angry with Abby I can't think straight? I am, okay," he admitted roughly. "I'm so mad at her right now that most days I can't bear to be in the same room as her. And the crazy thing is, half of what I'm feeling isn't even about my son. It's about *her*. It's always about Abby. I feel like I'm back in high school all over again. So yeah, I'm pissed."

"Because she married Tom?" Mitch guessed quietly.

Jake pushed a hand through his hair. "Because she didn't understand why I had to leave."

"I'm not sure any of us understood," Joss said.

Jake looked at Mitch. "You did."

Mitch nodded. "I knew you had to get the legacy of Billie-Jack out of your system. I knew you had to belong to something that wasn't about Cedar River, or this ranch, or even this family. I knew that once Billie-Jack left, nothing was keeping you here."

His brother, as usual, was right.

"I hated him," Jake admitted. "I still do."

"You're not the only one," Hank said quietly. "And we get it, you know. We saw how you always put yourself in the middle so that he wouldn't beat up on the rest of us."

Jake winced, remembering how often he'd taken a fist from his father that was meant for one of his brothers. And remembering that Hank had more reason to hate Billie-Jack than any of them. "It was all I could do."

"You mean, to prove you weren't anything like him?" Mitch suggested.

Jake shrugged. "I think my greatest fear was ending up like our father."

"I don't know what he's like now, and frankly, I don't care," Mitch said solemnly. "But I do know that back then, Billie-Jack was angry and resentful and weak. And Jake, you're nothing like that."

"Except around Abby," he admitted.

"It takes time, that's all," Mitch said and half smiled. "And now that you're back, you have time. You are back for good, correct?"

He nodded. "For as long as T.J. needs me."

"Don't forget that while you're so set on doing what's best for your son," his brother added, "you might want to consider what you need, too."

"I have no idea what I need," he said and sighed. "Or want."

"Abby?" Joss suggested. "At a guess."

Jake shook his head. "I can't resent her and want her at the same time. It's exhausting."

"Then pick a side," Joss teased.

"You ever had the one person you care about most in the world smash your heart to bits?"

"Yes," Mitch and Tess said simultaneously. Then they both laughed softly, and Tess grabbed his brother's hand. "I think what we mean," she said gently, "is that we all go through things we think we can never recover from… and yet, we do," she said and rubbed her belly. "I never imagined that your brother and I would be back in love with each other, married again and about to have a baby. But we are. And if I had to go through all that heartache again to get to where I am now, I would."

It was a nice story. But Tess and Mitch had the kind of love that transcended betrayal. "She kept my son a secret for six years," he reminded them.

"In plain sight," Joss said quietly.

Jake's gaze narrowed. "What?"

"She kept him in *plain sight*," Joss said again. "And really, any one of us could have guessed the truth had we taken the time to really look at the kid. He's the image of you, Jake. I mean, I suspected, so I could have said something… I could have asked her, or at least touched base with you and mentioned it. So yeah, maybe she didn't ac-tually *say* he was yours, but I didn't see her running away and hiding him from the world, either."

"Joss is right," Mitch added. "Knowing we all live in this town, she could have left, and none of us would have suspected a thing. But she didn't. She stayed. Why is that?"

"I've stopped trying to understand Abby's motives," he replied.

"Because you're still in love with her?" Joss said.

"Because there's no point," Jake said, refusing to in-criminate himself any further. "Abby and I are done—she made sure of that the moment she decided to marry Tom and then managed to pass my son off as his for six years."

"I was right," Joss said and shook his head. "You *are* a hard-ass…and an unforgiving one at that."

Jake knew there was truth in his brother's words. He'd hardened himself over the years, after enduring the worst of Billie-Jack's violent outbursts, after two tours in Iraq after losing the only woman he'd ever loved to his best friend…hardening his heart was the only way he knew how to get through.

"Look," he said with an impatient breath. "I appreci-ate everyone's concern, but I'm *fine*. Really. I only want to concentrate on my son and figuring out how be a par-ent. Abby isn't a part of that."

"Yeah," Joss said and chuckled. "That's why you moved in next door, right?"

"To be close to T.J. and not his mom. And I plan on buying a house as soon as possible," he said and pulled his keys from his pocket. "Thanks for your help with my car," he said to Joss. Using a couple of contacts, his brother had arranged collection and transportation of his Jeep from Sacramento and had had it dropped off at the ranch early that morning. He'd also taken Jake's bike to his auto re-pair shop for service.

He left after that, tired of hearing platitudes and advice and the sound of voices that had no clue about what he was going through. He detoured back into town, stopping at the supermarket for a few supplies before he headed back home. *Home.* It seemed odd thinking of the small apart-ment as home. He'd been thinking about getting some-thing more permanent now he'd made the decision to stay in Cedar River. Like a house. On the way through the main street he stopped at the local real estate office and picked up a flyer listing all the residential properties for sale in town. He stuffed it into his pocket and headed back to the Jeep just as snow started falling.

A white Christmas. The idea made him smile. It had been years since he'd experienced a holiday with snow. And he knew that T.J. would get a buzz out of the kid's-size snow boots he'd ordered from a store in town. Christmas was a little over a week away, and he was looking forward to the event more than he had in years. Maybe ever.

He pulled the Jeep into the driveway, quickly dropped the groceries off upstairs and then headed around the back toward Abby's place. The sun was just setting, and he was about the tap on the back door when he heard the familiar sound of his son's voice…although it was many decibels louder than usual.

Jake tapped on the door again, and when no one an-swered, opened the door and walked into the kitchen, catching the tail end of a conversation between Abby and T.J., that was echoing down from the hallway.

"But I want to, Mommy!"

Jake heard Abby's impatient response. "Not tonight," she said firmly.

"You never let me do anything," he wailed, and Jake

heard the loud bang of a door. "I hate you, Mommy! I hate you forever!"

When he reached the hallway, Jake spotted Abby standing outside T.J.'s bedroom. He said her name and she looked up. "Oh…hi."

"I did knock. Everything okay?" he asked, clearly knowing it wasn't.

She shrugged, and he didn't miss how her eyes were glistening with tears. "Just a disagreement about bedtime."

Jake checked his watch. "It's still early."

"I know," she replied and walked toward him, "but he said he wanted to stay up and watch something on television later tonight. I said no, and he had a tantrum."

Jake followed her steps back down the hall and into the kitchen. "Does this happen often?"

She shook her head and then nodded, dropping her hands to her sides. "More often than I like," she admitted.

"What kind of things does he say to you?" he asked quietly.

"Oh, you mean other than he hates me and I'm the worst mother in the world?"

Jake winced. "Well, we both know that's not true, Abby."

"Do we?" she remarked, and then sighed, but he heard the sound of tears in her voice. "I'm not so sure. I let him believe Tom was his father. I kept him from you for six years, as you've pointed out so often. So what kind of mother does that make me?"

"The protective kind," Jake assured her. "The kind who always puts him first."

"That's sweet of you to say," she said and shrugged. "But I think my past actions disprove that theory."

Sweet? Jake wasn't sure he'd ever been called that

before. And he suddenly had an urgent need to make her feel better. Stupid, he knew. The less he *felt* around Abby, the better. He remembered what his brother had said about her hiding their son in plain sight and realized it was true.

"If you'd truly wanted to keep T.J. a secret, Abby, you would have moved to Canada or something. And frankly, any one of my brothers could have figured out that T.J. was my kid if they'd looked close enough. He kind of looks like me."

She nodded, her expression softening. "And he has your birthmark. I couldn't believe it when he was first born and I saw that on his shoulder. He was so tiny but had so much fight inside him, so much courage and strength. Like you."

Jake's insides twitched. "I wish I'd been there with you."

"I wanted you there," she admitted shakily. "I just didn't know how to make it happen."

You could have called me…let me know I was a daddy with a baby fighting for his life…

Jake wanted to say it, but the words only hovered. Because as much as he was as mad as hell with Abby, he didn't like hurting her. And he didn't want their son hurting her, either.

"If it's okay with you, I'll go and talk with T.J. He needs to know it's not okay to say he hates you."

She stared at him. "He only—"

"Says it when he doesn't get his own way," Jake supplied, cutting her off. "Maybe, but it's still not acceptable. Not to me, and it shouldn't be to you, either."

Jake left the room, his throat unusually tight, his heart unsteady behind his ribs, his thoughts more jumbled than they'd ever been in his life.

* * *

Abby was still in the kitchen when T.J. came to see her half an hour later. Her son moved around the kitchen counter and hugged her around the waist, pressing his face into her belly. She rubbed the top of his head affectionately, and a great surge of love washed over her. And for Jake, too, because although she didn't know what had transpired between them, she suspected it had something to do with honor and respect and truth—things she knew were important to Jake.

"I'm sorry, Mommy."

"I know."

He hiccuped and sighed. "Daddy said I should never say mean things to the person who loves me more than anyone else in the whole world," he said and hugged her tighter.

Abby looked up and saw Jake standing in the doorway. He looked so handsome, her heart flipped over. She loved him so deeply but wasn't foolish enough to imagine those feelings were reciprocated. He was proving to be a wonderful father, and she loved him all the more for the way he'd embraced their son and fatherhood—but their relationship was well and truly over.

And I'm fine with that...

All that mattered was T.J. being successfully co-parented by two people who loved him. And she could clearly see how quickly Jake had formed a bond with their son. T.J. thought Jake hung the moon. Her son, she knew, had been yearning for a father, and seeing them together made it very clear how wrong she'd been in denying Jake the knowledge of his son.

She mouthed a thank-you to him, and he nodded, smiling a little. "Your daddy's right, but sometimes people do things without realizing they are hurting someone they love."

"Have you ever done that, Mommy?" T.J. asked and looked up.

Abby brushed his forehead and glanced toward Jake. "I'm sure I have."

"But you didn't mean it either, did you?" He asked the question with such innocence that Abby's whole body ached.

"No, honey, I didn't mean it," she said, not daring to look at Jake, because the raw emotion surging through her blood would make it obvious she was talking about him. *About them.*

"I love you, Mommy," her son said and hugged her.

"I love you, too," she said and smiled. "Now, how about you wash up for dinner?"

He nodded. "Is Daddy having dinner with us?"

She glanced toward Jake. "If he'd like to, of course he can."

T.J. turned toward his father. "Will you, Daddy?"

"Sure, buddy."

Abby's insides clenched. Of course, she knew spending time with Jake was part of their unofficial coparenting arrangement, and as much as part of her enjoyed his company, the other part ached inside thinking about how far removed from one another they really were. The tension was palpable. Unspoken words hung between them. And her dreams were plagued with images of him. Which meant most days she woke up restless and lethargic and spent her time as a hazy facsimile of the person she normally was. For years she'd lived her life in a kind of red alert, waiting for the day her secret would be exposed and Jake would discover the truth. And now that he had, nothing was as she'd expected. Oh, their relationship was just as she'd imagined it would be—a civil demonstration of two people trying to find a way to be parents to a child who clearly needed them both. But nothing else had really changed except for T.J. being happier than she'd ever seen him. When she'd made arrangements with the school to give Jake authority to be on the contact list and the school administrator had asked her directly what the relationship between Jake and T.J. was, she admitted the truth publicly for the first time. And her world didn't end. The sky didn't fall in. Yes, there had been questions and a natural curiosity. And she knew there would be talk. Cedar River was a small town and gossip was inevitable. But as long as she could protect her son from it, she would weather whatever happened. And she was sure Jake felt the same. When she had a meeting at work with Liam and Connie and told them, neither had seemed surprised. When she'd told a couple of friends, no one had had an overly surprised response. In fact, one of them had asked if she and Jake were back together, and when she'd made it clear they weren't, her friend had asked if she'd mind if she gave Jake a call. Which, of course, she did! But she felt she didn't have the right to say so. Jake was a single guy—he could do what he liked. And date who he wanted. Even if the idea hurt her down to her bones.

And through her week of sleeplessness, through her concerns that her beloved child would be tarred somehow as the illegitimate son of her husband's best friend, T.J. was flourishing. Her son loved his father. And clearly Jake loved his son. When she'd broached the idea of changing his last name to Culhane to T.J., her son had jumped at the idea without any reservations. Which amplified Abby's guilt tenfold. One, because T.J. was so desperate to have a flesh-and-blood father to call his own. And two, because Tom Perkins, his *angel daddy* and the man who'd taken place of pride on the mantel for so long, had now become secondary and T.J. had announced he wanted a picture of his *real* dad above the fireplace as well.

"Everything okay, Abby?"

She looked up and met Jake's glittering gaze. "What did you say to him?"

"Guy stuff," he replied and then half smiled. "Just that it's not okay to say you hate someone."

Abby grabbed plates from the cupboard. "Thank you, I appreciate it more than you could know. But," she added, "he'll hate me even more when he finds out I didn't tell you about him."

"He'll only know what we tell him, and for the moment that's enough," he said, and came around the counter. "I don't think we need to burden him with too much information."

"Who'd have thought that you'd end up being the voice of reason in this situation?" she said and offered brittle laughter that defied the anguish in her heart, and then she flapped a hand dismissively. "Ignore me, I'm just having an emotional breakdown."

"Ignore you?" he echoed, and took the plates from her hands. "Impossible. That would be like forgetting to breathe. And I don't think you're having a breakdown, Abby. You're too strong-willed and stubborn for that. But you do look exhausted. So why don't you sit down and let me cook dinner."

She gave him a look. "*You're* going to cook?"

He laughed, and the sound etched deep down into her soul. "I'm not completely inept in the kitchen, you know."

"I thought that's why you joined the military," she said, and passed him an apron. "So you'd get three square meals a day."

He took the apron and look down into her face. "You

know why I joined," he said soberly and then smiled a little. "The meals were a bonus."

"I didn't mean to sound trite. After what you said the other day, I'm beginning to understand," she admitted. She'd spent days going over the words. Days trying to fathom the fallout from what she had done and the decisions she had made.

"We said a lot of things the other day."

Memory of their heated conversation bombarded her thoughts. They had said a lot of things. And they'd kissed. And argued. It seemed to be the tempo of their relationship.

"I feel guilty," she said and sighed. "Which you know, of course. And not just because I didn't tell you about T.J., but about Tom."

"Why?"

"Because I could never truly regret what happened between us. That would mean I regretted T.J.'s existence—and I don't. I mean, how could I? He's the most precious gift in the world. But there have been times when the guilt was almost all-consuming, if that makes sense. I started referring to Tom as his angel daddy to make the inevitable transition easier."

"What inevitable transition?"

"You," she replied. "Coming back to Cedar River. Learning the truth about you being his father. All of it."

His gaze narrowed. "You mean you *did* intend to tell me?"

She nodded. "Yes. But then, things got complicated and we started…you know…to reconnect. It's no excuse, but that's the truth. I wanted to tell you that night I asked you to meet me at the Loose Moose. I chickened out because I'm a coward."

"You're not a coward, Abby," he said gently. "You're a protective mom. And a good one."

"Perhaps," she said and sighed. "But I'm not sure I was such a great wife. To T.J., Tom's always been a picture above a fireplace, a father-figure he could call his own, and now Tom's fading from T.J.'s thoughts. It makes me feel such sadness, and shame, because he got a raw deal when he married me."

"Tom loved you," Jake said quietly. "He knew what he was doing."

"Did he? I hope so. I hope he didn't marry me simply because I was the first girl who'd said yes. The truth is, he loved us both. But once you left town, he asked me out pretty much right away. I said no, of course, that it was too soon, that I still wasn't…over you. I used to wonder if he pursued me because he wanted to compete with you. It's illogical, I guess, and doesn't make a bit of difference now…but he had to have a reason for wanting me."

Jake grabbed her hand. "Other than the fact that you're beautiful and smart and funny and great to be around?"

Abby looked at where their hands were linked. He was so close. And he smelled so good.

"Maybe I was those things once," she said quietly. "I'm pretty sure you don't think I'm so great to be around these days."

He dropped her hand. "At times. Goes with the territory, I guess."

"The one that sits between anger and betrayal, you mean?"

His gaze was unwavering. "Exactly. Abby, Tom's gone," he reminded her, his voice even, "but I don't see the harm in keeping his memory alive for T.J."

"But I thought you might be—"

"What?" he asked, cutting her off. "Jealous? Insecure?"

He shook his head. "I'm not. And while I'm still trying to rationalize your reasons for keeping the truth from me, I'm not unhappy that my son has had the memory of a good man to look up to."

Abby stilled, her heart beating so fast she could barely breathe. "Thank you. I appreciate that you're being so understanding."

"Like Patience said, we have to get along for our son's sake."

She nodded and pulled the tray of fried chicken from the refrigerator. "These need reheating, and there's a potato bake in the microwave."

"Great," he said and laughed. "Because my cooking is terrible."

But his kisses were out of this world...

Abby shook her thoughts off and moved around him. "There's a car in my grandmother's driveway," she said as she looked out of the window.

"My car," he supplied. "I had it sent from Sacramento."

She nodded. "Looks like you're here to stay."

Jake gaze narrowed. "I told you I was staying, Abby. All I need to do now is buy a house."

She raised a brow. "Is Gran's small apartment cramping your style?"

He stared at her. "What does that mean?"

Abby shrugged. "One of my friends asked me if you were seeing anyone at the moment. I said I had no idea. I can get her number if you'd like."

He stopped what he was doing. "I'm not interested."

Abby ignored a tiny surge of triumph and shrugged again, moving to the other side of the counter. "You'll need a booster seat for the back."

"Already have one," he replied. "I thought I'd take him Christmas shopping tomorrow, if that's okay with you?"

"Perfectly," she replied. "Just don't spoil him, okay," she said and then waved her hand. "Okay, you can spoil him if you like. But honestly, he's happy to simply hang out with you."

He nodded. "I like that, too. And thank you for sorting out the arrangement with the school. I appreciate it."

"No problem. Also, he's over the moon at the idea of being T.J. Culhane. I thought that when the next school term starts we could make the transition. It will obviously mean some intrusive questions from certain people—but I think he can handle it."

"What about you?"

Abby gave a startled gasp. "What?"

"You plan on changing your name back to Reed?"

Her pounding heart subsided. "Ah…not immediately. I'll change it if I get married again."

She watched as he wrapped the apron around his waist, looking totally masculine and so sexy it defied words. She didn't want to talk about marriage with Jake. And the idea he might marry someone one day made her ache all over.

"I suppose you'd like more kids?" he asked as he worked on preparing their food.

Heat crawled up her neck. "One day. Before the clock starts ticking too loudly."

He tilted his head a fraction. "You're still young."

Abby shrugged. "I'm nearly thirty-two. It's moot anyhow, since I'm not seeing anyone at the moment…well, you know, except…"

You…

The word stuck, and she moved away, grabbing the plates and setting the table just as T.J. came back into the room.

"Daddy," he announced, saying it as though he'd been

saying it all his life, "can we play a video game after dinner?"

Jake looked at her, and she nodded. "Sure, but remember you have school tomorrow, so we can't stay up too late."

"I remember. Are you coming to my Christmas concert?"

"Wouldn't miss it."

T.J.'s beaming face filled Abby with so much love. He was so happy it made every ounce of her own misery worth suffering. The concert was on Thursday afternoon, and she'd made arrangements to finish work early so she could help with the costumes. She knew Mitch and Tess were coming also, and Joss, since his girls were both performing at the event. It would be her first public outing since Jake had discovered the truth about their son, and although she knew the Culhanes had embraced the knowledge that T.J. was one of them, she had no idea how they would react to her. Civilly, of course. But she suspected there might be resentment also. And they would close ranks around Jake because he was family. And T.J. was family, too.

It was Abby who was the outsider.

Which became very evident to her the following day when her son announced that he wanted to spend Christmas at the Triple C Ranch with his father and uncles and aunt and cousins.

And for the first time in his young life, not with her.

Chapter Eleven

The Cedar River Elementary School Christmas concert was not something Jake had consciously thought he'd ever be attending. Nor did he ever think he'd be one of the proud parents, sitting in the second row, watching his son perform a melody of Christmas carols with a group of other six-year-olds, wearing a reindeer costume. His brother Joss sat to his left, and Tess was to his right, while Mitch had the aisle seat so he could stretch out his cast.

The concert was in full swing, the young voices echoing around the auditorium, and the place was filled with delighted parents and grandparents and caregivers and guardians. In all his life, Jake couldn't remember experiencing a moment that gave such complete and utter pride and joy.

My son...

His pride was only overshadowed by his growing love for the little boy who made him want to be the best possible version of himself. He'd heard about how life changing parenthood was, from his friends, from the men and women he served with in the military, and from his brother Joss. But he'd never, for one moment, imagined he could feel anything so profoundly. He'd willingly gone to war and would have given his life for his country. He'd put himself between his siblings and their drunken father time and time again to keep them from harm. And now, he knew he would protect his son with his life, his soul, his very being, until the end of time.

He spotted Abby in the wings, helping the kids with their costumes. She'd been unusually quiet for the past few days, and although he'd tried several times to find out why, she'd shut him down and insisted she was fine. But he wasn't convinced. Abby was unhappy, and Jake knew that he was the reason. He didn't mean to be. He wanted to get along with her, despite the turmoil she created in his head and heart.

Once the song was over, there was a short break as the kids disappeared offstage to change for their next number. He remained in his seat, but Jake was acutely aware of Abby on the sidelines.

"Having fun?" Joss asked and jabbed him in the ribs.

"Actually," he said over the sound of the band, "I am."

"Mitch said you bought a house?"

He nodded, thinking about the deal he'd signed that morning. "Down by the river."

"On Millionare's Row?"

He half-smiled at his brother's words. He knew the spot was considered some of the best real estate in the area, but he'd lucked upon a motivated seller and got the place for a good price. "It's a nice house."

"Big enough for a family I suppose?" Joss quizzed.

He shrugged. "I guess."

"What did Abby say about it?"

"I haven't told her yet."

Joss grinned. "Chicken."

"It's no secret that I wanted to buy a house," he said and ignored the heat clumbing up his neck. "As convenient as it is living next door, we need to get a routine in place for T.J."

"I'm really proud of you," Joss said and then grinned again. "I know that's stupid because you're older than me, but you've really stepped up to fatherhood."

"I'm not sure that's a compliment or what. Did you doubt that I would?"

"Nah," Joss said and chuckled. "You're one of those annoying people who are good at everything you do."

Except forgiving the woman I love...

Jake shook off the thought. He knew he had to stop thinking about Abby that way. They were over. She was his son's mother, nothing more. But spending time with her had only amplified the feelings he'd managed to push aside for the last fourteen years. Feelings that had never truly disappeared, which was no doubt why they made love after Tom's funeral. Funny, but he'd never been able to think of being with Abby as just sex. He'd *had* sex with other women, and it had been pleasurable, and yet the emptiness of it always stayed with him afterward. But Abby...was different. She was his first love. Being with her after his brother's wedding had only brought all those feelings back. The memory of a touch that transcended the erotic, of a kiss that was more than lips against lips, of the joining of bodies that somehow felt more spiritual than physical. He felt stupid thinking it, imagining what they shared was more than simple hooking up. But the memory stayed with him.

Once the show was over, the parents and friends were all invited to a light buffet hosted by the faculty. Jake left his brothers and went searching for Abby. He found her with T.J., chatting with a woman he quickly discovered was his son's teacher.

"Mr. Culhane." The fiftysomething woman, whom Abby introduced as Mrs. Santino, spoke quietly, treating Jake as though he'd always been known as T.J.'s father— as though there was nothing unusual about his sudden appearance in his son's life. "T.J. has been telling me about the snowboarding lessons you've been giving him."

Jake ruffled his son's hair. "He's a natural. We'll be boarding down Kegg's Mountain before we know it."

"Really, Daddy?"

"Sure, buddy," he said, seeing Abby's horrified expression, and he touched her arm. "Relax, he'll be perfectly safe."

"Yeah, Mommy," T.J. said and giggled. "Daddy will look after me."

There was such faith and confidence in his son's words that Jake felt as though his heart was being squeezed. "We'll make sure Mommy's there to supervise, okay?"

They spoke with the teacher for a few minutes, and then T.J. said he wanted some cake, so they headed for the buffet. David's son Jasper was there, and T.J. was quickly distracted as the boys talked about their latest video game.

"Everything okay, Abby?" Jake asked as he passed her some punch. .

She took the paper cup. "I'm good. Relieved the concert went off without a hitch. He's been so worried he'd forget the words to the songs."

"His teacher seems nice."

"She is," Abby said. "He adores school most days, which is one less hurdle. I know plenty of parents who have a real battle to get their kids ready in the morning. Lucky for us he loves to learn."

"You've done an amazing job raising him. And although this is probably not the place for this discussion," he said quietly, "we need to talk about some kind of financial arrangement for him."

Her gaze narrowed. "I don't want your money. And you're right, this *isn't* the place."

Jake grasped her elbow and ushered her closer. "Okay, but we'll talk about this later."

He didn't say anything more as Patience walked up

to them and suggested they head home. Jake had driven them together and quickly agreed to drive them home. He said a quick goodbye to his brothers before they left and figured they were thinking the scene smacked of domesticity, which it probably did, since he bundled his son and his child's mother *and* grandmother into his Jeep. Patience and T.J. chatted tirelessly on the trip home, while Abby was conspicuously quiet.

When he pulled up in the driveway, Patience tapped him on the shoulder. "Jake, be a dear while I'm away and feed my goldfish, will you?" she asked. "The spare key is under the flowerpot on the back porch."

Patience was heading to Florida the next day to visit her daughter over the holidays as usual and would be gone for a week. Jake knew that Abby and T.J. usually accompanied her. He also knew that Abby had elected to stay in Cedar River so he could spend some of the holiday break with his son. Which included sleeping over at the ranch on Christmas Eve. Once T.J. had learned that Joss's daughters were staying at the ranch with their father, and that Grant would be there along with Ellie and Mitch and Tess, his son had made his wishes very clear. He wanted the same experience as his newly discovered cousins—to wake up at the ranch, to go for an early pony ride, to play with the toys he knew were already wrapped under the big tree. Jake had taken T.J. to the ranch several times in the past couple of weeks, and he knew how much his son had come to love the place. He felt T.J.'s excitement and sense of inclusion, particularly when Tess told him they had saved a special spot for his picture along the wide stairway where all the family photographs hung.

But he also knew what it meant for Abby.

"Of course," he replied. "Happy to help."

Patience was quickly out of the car and T.J. followed,

saying he had to collect a book that he'd left at his grandmother's. Jake waited for Abby to move, but she remained where she was, her breathing heavy, her gaze straight ahead.

"Something on your mind?" he asked.

"I meant what I said," she replied tightly. "I have no intention of taking money from you."

"Don't be ridiculous, Abby. You'd have to know I'd want to provide for my son."

"He needs your time, Jake, not your money."

"He's my son and my responsibility. That includes being financially responsible."

She turned her head and glared at him. "I've managed to provide for him quite adequately for the last six years, and I'll continue to do so."

"You're just being stubborn because you think I'm trying to be controlling. But I'm not. I actually would like to make things financially easier for you, too. That way you could cut back your hours at the hotel."

"So now you think I work too much?"

He sighed heavily, his hands still on the steering wheel. "No…that's not what I mean. Is this about Christmas?"

"Christmas?"

"About T.J. wanting to spend the holidays at the ranch?"

She turned in the seat. "This is about you thinking you can waltz into this situation and do whatever you want."

"That's not what I think," he said incredulously.

"I'm pretty sure it is," she snapped. "And I get it—I have some serious ground to make up and being extra accomodating is my medicine. So, I'll take it. To a degree. I have a career I love and a well paying position at the hotel—I don't need your money."

Jake inhaled a long breath. "I hear you, and of course I respect your opinion and your career. However, he's my son, and I want to support him—that means everything from the clothes on his back today to a car when he's sixteen and a college fund when he finishes high school. Everything I've worked for, that's his legacy, Abby. And as for Christmas—"

"This isn't about Christmas," she said, cutting him off. "I'm happy to do whatever my son asks for. He wants to spend time with you, and I fully support that."

"You're sure?"

She grabbed the door handle. "Positive. Thanks for the lift. I know T.J. appreciated having us all there together like..."

A family...

Jake felt the words but didn't hear them. And he wasn't about to verbalize them.

He knew what she was thinking—there had been times in the past couple of weeks that he'd managed to suppress his resentment and think about the situation logically. There was an element of family about their situation.

But he wasn't about to start thinking it was anything more than that—particularly for his son's sake. He didn't want T.J. getting any ideas that they were about to set up house together and start playing mom and dad and acting as though their situation was normal. Not that there was a *normal*. He knew several couples who successfully coparented without being together. Families came in all shapes and sizes, and there was no perfect, stock-standard formula for raising kids. He figured that he and Abby would simply do the best they could. In the meantime, he had some changes to make.

"I bought a house," he said quietly.

Her eyes widened. "That was quick."

He shrugged. "It's been on the market for a while and the owners wanted a quick sale. It's down by the river. It's got four bedrooms, a jetty and a boathouse. I think T.J.

will like it. If you're free tomorrow, perhaps you would like to come with me and check it out?"

She frowned. "Ah…it's really not my business where you decide to live."

"It is, since our son will be spending time there."

She nodded warily. "Okay. I finish work at one o'clock."

"I'll talk to the Realtor and see if she can meet us there since I obviously don't have the keys yet. I'll pick you up and drop you off before it's school pickup time. I offered to take your grandmother to Rapid City to catch her flight, but she said she'd prefer to leave her car at the airport for the time she's away."

"Gran has an independent streak," Abby remarked.

Jake half smiled. "Runs in the family, huh?"

She made a face. "Will you be coming by later to tuck him in?"

Jake nodded. Story time with T.J., before tucking him in for the night, had become something of a tradition. "Yep. See you at eight."

She grabbed her tote and the bag containing their son's discarded reindeer costume and walked up to the house. Jake sat in the Jeep for several minutes. Thinking. Wondering. And realized he had no clue how to compartmentalize his feelings for Abby.

He also realized he was tired of trying.

"I don't want to leave you alone."

Abby hugged her grandmother. "Don't worry about me, Gran. I'll be fine. And I won't be alone."

Actually, I will.

Because T.J. would be going to the Triple C with his father on Christmas Eve and wouldn't be back until the following afternoon. Even *that* was a negotiation with her son, as he would have been more than happy to spend several days at the ranch hanging out with his new family.

"I feel like I should stay," Patience said and hugged her tighter.

"Mom's expecting you," she reminded her. "And once I explained why I couldn't come this year, she completely understood. Like you, she's been telling me I should have come clean to Jake for years. And you were both right. Now that Jake knows, things were bound to change."

"But you'll be alone on Christmas morning," Patience said and smiled sadly. "I can't imagine how awful that will be for you."

"If I don't think I can handle it, I'll tell Liam I want to work an extra shift that day. But I'm fine," she insisted. "Honestly. Stop worrying about me and go and see Mom and enjoy the lovely warm weather while you can. You know the winter always gets bad after the holidays."

"I'm more concerned about you at the moment."

It took another ten minutes of cajoling to get her grandmother to leave, but finally she waved her off in her small car, with both T.J. and Jake at her side. Of course, neither male had been privy to the conversation she'd had with Patience. Firstly, because she didn't want T.J. getting an inkling that she wasn't completely okay with not being able to spend all of the holidays with him. And secondly, because she didn't want Jake's pity—which was inevitable if he suspected she was upset by the idea of having her first Christmas morning without her son. She was trying to take the high road, to accept the consequences of her actions. Her son, who meant everything to her in the world, wanted to be with his father, and she had to accept that and give him every opportunity to do so.

"Who wants pancakes?" she offered, a wide smile plastered on her face.

T.J. jumped up and down with an excited yes, but Jake declined, citing work and an early conference call with his business partner. He reaffirmed their arrangement to meet that afternoon and disappeared to his apartment. After breakfast, she dropped T.J. at school and headed for the hotel. The breakfast shift was busy, and she was exhausted by the time the lunch chef turned up. She tidied herself up a little before one o'clock, changing her shirt and reapplying her lip gloss. Jake was in the foyer well before one, talking with Connie. He smiled when he spotted her walking toward them, and her heart skipped a beat crazily. She wondered if she'd ever stop feeling that. If the attraction between them would ever wane. Perhaps not. Perhaps first love was always the hardest to endure.

They were in his Jeep and on the road a little after one, heading across the bridge and toward the exclusive properties that ran along the river.

"Liam lives down this way," she commented as they passed a few discreet driveways.

"Actually," Jake said as he turned the vehicle into a driveway that had a huge For Sale sign out front, "he lives next door. But this property sits on a little over three acres, so there's plenty of privacy."

"Are you planning on having wild parties that require privacy?"

He frowned and pulled up. "I've never been a bed hopper, Abby. But you seem to want to think the worst of me. Have I been a saint these past few years? No. But I haven't been leaving behind a trail of broken hearts or broken promises, either. I like sex as much as the next person, but I'd rather you didn't accuse me of being some kind of man whore when I'm not."

"I don't think that," she said, horrified he would suggest such a thing, because it made her sound like a jealous, judgmental prig. "I'm sorry. I guess we really don't know each other that well any more. High school was a long time ago."

"You know me," he said, and then hesitated for a moment. "And I suspect neither of us have changed all that much over the years."

His got out without another word and came around to the passenger side, holding the door wider as she got out. She grabbed her bag once her feet were on the ground and looked around.

"Wow," she said and gave a soft whistle. "This is amazing."

The house was big and designed to have a fabulous view of the river and the mountains beyond. In three levels, it was constructed from split timber, and had long glass windows opening onto a huge veranda.

Another car came barreling down the driveway and Abby recognized the local Realtor's logo on the side of the vehicle. A woman got out and after a brief introduction, the house was unlocked and they were shown inside.

Abby didn't stop oohing for the next ten minutes. The house was incredible, designed to have optimal views. The master suite was on the highest level, while the remaining bedrooms and kitchen and living area were in the middle, and the huge gaming room and office were on the ground floor. The kitchen was a chef's dream. Solid marble countertops, Shaker-style cabinets, top-of-the-line stainless steel appliances—Abby felt like she was in her dream home.

"What do you think?" he asked as they headed up the stairway for the top floor, while the Realtor walked back outside—obviously giving them privacy, and probably misinterpreting their relationhip.

"It's incredible," she replied as they entered the master suite, and then she stopped in her tracks. Built into the wall and sporting a magnificent view was a huge bed, perhaps the biggest she'd ever seen.

"The bed comes with the house," he explained, clearly interpreting her surprise. "It's attached to the wall."

"So I see," she said and averted her gaze, refusing to think about Jake being sprawled out on the bed. She moved around the room and checked out the bathroom, which was spectacular, and then stood by the doors that led to the veranda and looked out over the river. "It's a lovely house."

"Do you think T.J. will be happy here?"

She turned, noticing he was barely a few feet behind her. "I'm sure he'll be happy wherever you are."

"I'm really proud to be his dad, you know."

She didn't dare look at him, because emotion was clogging her throat. Jake could give their son everything he wanted, including the fatherly love and affection T.J. had craved for so long. It filled her with such conflict, and that transcended into guilt of the worse kind—because the guilt tasted an awful lot like jealousy. And since she'd never been the jealous type, it created more conflict within her. Everything about her relationship with Jake confused and tormented her. She knew she had to get over it. She just didn't know how.

"He loves you, Jake," she said softly. "The truth is, I've never seen him so happy. And that makes me happy."

"Does it?" he queried. "Even though you have to share him now?"

Abby met his intuitive gaze. "Even then. I know things are changing, and yes, I'm probably not so great at handling change, but I'm learning. I'm determined to make this coparenting thing work."

"It's nothing like I imagined."

"What is?" she asked.

"Loving a child."

The raw honestly is his voice cut her through to the quick. "I know."

"Every time he calls me Daddy, I just have this over-whelming sensation that I can't even put into words."

Abby's eyes burned and she blinked hard, feeling emotion sweep though her body. And then the tears came, filling her eyes and then spilling down her cheeks. She walked closer toward the window, noticing snow on the mountains and the ripples from a lone boat out on the river. It was an incredibly peaceful spot, and she knew her son would be happy spending time by the boathouse with his father. If she looked closely enough, she could almost see them together, laughing and talking, being the tight unit she suspected would grow deeper over time. T.J. would learn so much from his father—like how to be a strong and ethical person, how to care for the people he loved, how to show courage and fortitude, how to be a good friend and, more importantly, a good man.

Once Jake moved into the house, T.J. would visit regularly, perhaps preferring the home to the one he shared with her. And Abby would have to let him go. She would have to learn selflessness. To be the mother she should have been the moment she'd discovered she was pregnant—and the woman who should have told Jake the truth from the beginning.

"I wish I could have a do-over," she said quietly, wiping the tears from her cheeks. "I'd make so many different choices."

"Like what?" he asked.

"You know what," she replied and shuddered.

Jake was in front of her in two strides. He grabbed her hands, holding them tightly in his own. "I would have been there, Abby," he said quietly, his voice so raw she felt fresh tears fill her eyes. "I would have been beside you when he was born. I would have held your hand every minute he was in the hospital."

"I know. I wanted you there," she admitted and couldn't help the sob that racked through her body. "I wanted you there so much."

He quickly gathered her close, running his strong hands down her back and holding her against him. Abby stiffened for a moment but then relaxed. There was something cathartic about his touch, about the gentleness of his embrace, about the soothing sound of his voice. The scent of him was achingly familiar, and his strong arms were like a cloak, holding her safely, keeping her pain and heartache at bay.

One hand rested against her nape, and he spoke softly. "You're okay."

Abby wept louder, part of her not even sure why she was in such a state. Guilt, she figured. And shame. And the knowledge that she loved a man who would never love her again. Because once, she'd had his heart, but her pride and stubbornness had made her toss it away. She'd broken them. She'd devalued everything they had once been to one another because she didn't get her own way. Then she married Tom—as a way to punish Jake for daring to live his own life.

So arrogantly...

So hurtfully...

In the end, the person who'd hurt most was herself.

And the child she loved more than life itself but whom she'd also punished because she was too selfish to admit what she had become—a self-pitying fool. And a self-important one. A woman who believed *her* thoughts and feelings were all that mattered. She'd made the decision for them both. For them *all*. Out of spite. Out of revenge. Out of her insatiable need to prove to herself that she was right—that Jake had chosen the military over her and them. That he would never come back. That she would end up just like her mother—heartbroken and grieving lost love. And that she was justified. She was right in her beliefs.

The realization and acknowledgment made her feel as small as she could possibly feel.

"I'm sorry, Jake. For everything."

"I know," he said quietly. If he'd kissed her, if he'd touched her, she would have gone with him willingly into a place where only the two of them existed.

But he didn't. Because her apology would never be enough. Abby felt it as surely as she breathed.

He still held her for a few moments, smoothing back her hair, saying very little but giving her the comfort she suddenly and desperately craved. The kind of comfort she'd only ever found in Jake's arms. That's why they'd made love after Tom's funeral. Because they'd needed one another. She'd needed Jake like she needed air in her lungs. Nothing and no one had ever come close to the feelings he evoked. He was the father of her child. And the love of her life.

She wondered if he'd somehow sensed her feelings, because he released her abruptly. Because, of course, he wouldn't want them. He didn't think of her that way. Perhaps if she'd shown enough gumption to tell him about T.J. instead of him finding out as he had, by accident, in front of his brother. Perhaps then things might have turned out differently. They might have dated—they *might* have done so many things.

"We should go," he said and stepped back. "I'll drive you back to the hotel. It's nearly time to pick up T.J. from school."

Abby wiped her eyes and quickly pulled herself together. "Of course. And Jake, the house is lovely. I'm sure you'll make this a happy home for T.J."

And for the next woman you love.

The very notion hurt her so profoundly she winced. Imagining Jake in love, thinking about him setting up house and making a family with someone, actually made her physically ache. But she knew it was in the future. Jake *would* get married one day. He'd find someone he trusted, someone who wouldn't marry his best friend, someone who wouldn't lie to him and steal six years of his child's life. He would probably have more children, and he'd be exactly what she'd always wanted—the kind of husband who was strong and dependable and loyal. Except he would be someone else's husband. The father of someone's else's children. And someone else's lover.

The trip back to the hotel was mainly silent. Abby was as wound up as a spring, and she sensed that Jake was no better. Abby grabbed her tote and the door handle simultaneously.

"I'll see you later," she said.

Jake gently grasped her arm. "Abby...wait..."

"What?"

"I never..." He paused, expelling a heavy breath. "I feel as though we never finish any conversation we start."

She didn't respond immediately. Didn't move. But she felt his hand against her skin like a branding iron and instinctively covered his hand with her own. "Habit. History. Take your pick."

He sighed. "We have to find a way to make this work."

"I thought we already had," she replied. "You can see T.J. as often as you want to. I'm not going to make things difficult. I know what I've done in the past was unfair to you both, and I've accepted that my son needs *and* wants his father. We both know that he has to come first. As for me?" She shrugged listlessly. "I'll learn to live with my mistakes. From breaking up with you in high school because you had the audacity to live your own life," she admitted and laughed brittlely. "To marrying a man who deserved way more than my misguided attempt to punish *you* for leaving. And mostly—" she wiped away a silent tear "—for denying you the right to be a father. I have a lot to make up for and a lot to be ashamed of."

He didn't disagree. Didn't say anything. And Abby knew she had truly lost him.

She'd lost him to betrayal. To selfishness. To arrogance.

And in a way, she'd lost T.J., too. Because her son would never be *only* hers again. He would have divided loyalties. She knew he would always love her, but his hero worship for Jake was only going to get stronger over the years, and he would stop needing her as much, stop relying on her. He'd already begun making choices—like Christmas. He wanted to be at the ranch. He wanted to be with his cousins and wake up Christmas morning with his kin.

And she would be alone.

Chapter Twelve

Jake looked at the gift on the table, considered unwrapping it for the millionth time and then pushed it aside. Maybe the smart thing would be to take it back to the store. He wasn't even sure why he'd bought the damn thing. It was for Abby. It was jewelry. Not a ring, even though the thought had stupidly crossed his mind when he was in the store. It was a gold chain and diamond pendant. It was overpriced, but he hadn't quibbled with the clerk. The truth was, he couldn't get out of the store fast enough, thinking that someone might see him and ask him what he was thinking.

Which was...

I don't have a freaking clue.

Sure, he'd purchased something for T.J. to give his mom, but he hadn't imagined he'd be foolish enough to buy a gift from himself. And it wasn't as though his son had encouraged him too much. It was all his own doing.

"What's that?"

Jake looked up. Mitch was standing in the doorway, still using crutches but looking a hell of a lot better than he had six weeks earlier. Jake grabbed the small parcel and put it in his jacket pocket. "Nothing."

Mitch laughed. "Secret, huh?"

"None of your business," he replied.

"What time is T.J. getting here?" Mitch asked, ignoring his scowl.

Jake glanced at the clock on the wall and saw it was nearly eleven. "Soon. His mother is dropping him off."

Mitch's brows both came up. "Things so bad you can't even say her name now?"

"What?"

"Exactly," his brother said. "You've been referring to her as *T.J.'s mom* all week."

"Easier," he quipped. "And I don't want to—"

"I know what you *don't* want," Mitch said pointedly as he sat down and stretched out his cast. "The question is, what is it that you *do* want?"

"Honestly," he replied. "I have no idea."

"Do you remember when you first got back to town," Mitch commented and tapped his fingers on the table. "You asked me what I was afraid of…why I was so determined to keep Tess at arm's length even though she's having my baby and I was still crazy in love with her. Pride… remember? So, now I'm asking you the same thing. Is your pride more important than how you feel about her?"

"It's not about pride," he replied. "It's about trust."

"You sure?"

Jake ran a hand through his hair. "I'm not sure about anything. How I feel…how *Abby* feels," he said, saying her name deliberately. "Truthfully, I've never been more conflicted in my life. I want to be a good dad. I want to make a difference in my son's life. And Abby…" He paused, trying to make sense of his brother's words, his own words, anything that Abby had said to him over the past few weeks, and as always, came up with more questions than answers, more confusion than clarity. And an ache the size of Mount Rushmore in the middle of his chest.

"She made a mistake," Mitch said quietly. "Who hasn't? Not me…and I'm betting not you, either."

"I can't…"

"Or won't," Mitch insisted. "Like I said, pride. She busted your pride, she chose another man, she had your son and didn't tell you. She did a lot of things, Jake…but so did you. You left town, you left us all…and then you came back when your best friend died and got his widow pregnant. So maybe you shouldn't be so quick to pass out judgment."

Jake stared at Mitch and registered the reproach in his voice. It was first real criticism he'd ever heard from his brother. "You think I should forgive her?"

"I think love and forgiveness go hand in hand," Mitch replied. "I think we've all gone through crap and have had to get past it. Things like everything we went through with Mom dying and Billie-Jack being a drunken bastard. Like how Tess miscarried four times and how it nearly ended us, but we still managed to find our way back together. Like how Hank almost died in the accident Billie-Jack caused, and yet he survived the accident and all those operations afterwards. Or how about how Joss picked up the pieces of his life after Lara died because he had two kids to raise. Or how Grant and Ellie had to grow up without parents—what I'm trying to say is that life's too short to waste on regret or grief or blame."

"He's right."

It was Joss's voice he heard from the doorway, and his younger brother was nodding. "I could have checked out when Lara died…you know how her folks wanted custody of the girls. I was twenty-four and didn't know what I was doing. But I had to man up and be responsible, and that included admitting I had to get on with my life."

"Is that why you've nailed everything in a skirt in this town and the next," Jake shot back and then quickly got to his feet. "Sorry, I didn't mean that. Ignore me, I'm going through some weird phase."

"We know," Joss said and smirked.

"Hey, Jake," Tess said and peered around the doorway. "Abby's here."

He straightened his back, looked at both his brothers and nodded. "Thanks for the talk."

Jake walked past Tess and headed down the hallway. He opened the front door and spotted Abby's Honda in the driveway. She was by the trunk, with T.J. at her side, removing a bag from the car. She looked so beautiful in a long denim skirt, bright blue sweater, black coat and scarf. Her hair was loose and flowed around her shoulders, but he could see the tension in her back. She was unhappy. Well, she wasn't the only one.

"Daddy!" T.J.'s excited voice rang out, and within seconds his son was racing toward him.

Jake met him at the bottom of the stairs and hauled him into his arms, swinging him around once before settling him back onto his feet. "Hey, buddy."

"It's almost Christmas," his son announced. "And I've been good, I promise."

Jake had given T.J. a serious talk about being good after his tantrum over bedtime, and since then his son had been mostly well behaved and respectful toward his mother. "Happy to hear it," he said and ruffled T.J.'s hair.

"Are my cousins here yet?" he asked hopefully.

Jake nodded. "They're inside. But I think Sissy wants to ride her new pony later today, so how about we all go down to the corral together and you can have a pony ride?"

"Yay!" he said and then turned as Abby walked toward them. "Did you hear that, Mommy? I'm gonna ride a pony!"

"That sounds wonderful," she said as she reached the bottom step.

"Can I go inside now?" he asked. "I wanna see everybody."

"Okay," Abby said and smiled. "So, I'll see you tomorrow?"

"Sure, Mommy," he replied and began to walk up the stairs.

Jake saw the pained expression on Abby's face and spoke quickly. "T.J., how about you give Mommy a kiss goodbye?"

Their son turned on his heels. "Oh, okay," he said and was quickly back down the steps. He hugged his mother, and Jake noticed how her hands lingered on his small shoulders, as though she couldn't bear the thought of letting him go.

Then he was gone, up the steps and into the house without a backward glance.

"He's excited," Jake said quietly.

"I know," she said and held out a small overnight bag. "His pajamas and a change of clothes for tomorrow," she explained as he took the bag. "And I put some emergency pants in there, too. And his favorite teddy. And a couple of books. And his toothbrush."

She really did think of everything. "Great. So, I'll see you tomorrow. I'll drop him off in the morning."

"He wants to stay until the afternoon," she said quietly.

Jake suspected those were some of the hardest words she'd ever said. "I'll bring him back in the morning," he said again. "As agreed."

She nodded. "Okay, thank you."

Jake gripped the bag. "Abby… I know this must be hard for you."

She shrugged loosely. "It's what T.J. wants."

"Perhaps," he agreed. "But it's still difficult. I know he's the most important thing in your life. And I know this is the first Christmas you'll be without him."

She stared at him and swallowed hard. "Like I said, this is what he wants. And I owe him the opportunity to spend as much time with you and your family as he asks for."

It sounded as though she was trying to convince herself, and they both knew it. "All I'm trying to say is that I understand. Listen, why don't you come inside for a while?"

"No."

He could see the tension tightening her mouth. "I'm sure everyone would like to—"

"I can't," she said swiftly and stepped back. "I picked up a shift at the restaurant. Another time, perhaps. I'll see you tomorrow."

"Abby..."

Jake didn't say anything else. He couldn't. Instead, he stared at her, seeing the girl he'd once loved and the woman he desperately wanted to hate. He thought about what his brothers had said—about pride—and realized they were right. He'd been keeping her at arm's length since he'd found out the truth about T.J. because his pride was battered, because he'd felt humiliated and belittled and wanted to punish her for denying him the right to be a father to his son. Like she'd punished him by marrying Tom. Payback, he thought. Worse than pride. A small man's revenge. In that moment, Jake felt smaller than he ever had in his life.

"I don't want us to be enemies," he said softly.

Her eyes widened. "Then what *do* you want?"

"I want... I want..." His words trailed off with a heavy sigh. "I want things to be different. But I..."

She met his gaze. "Jake?"

He stilled. "What?"

She took a long breath. "Do you know why I love him so much?"

"Huh?"

"T.J.," she said and gave a tremulous half smile. "Do you know why I love him so much?"

Jake stared at her, thinking there was something unusual about the way she was watching him. And he knew why—because T.J. was her whole life, her child, her baby. "Because he's your son," he said quietly.

She took a second, inhaling with a kind of uneasy shudder before she spoke again. "No, that's not why," she said. "I love him so much because he's *your* son."

Jake's breath stuck in his throat. "Abby... I..."

"Merry Christmas, Jake," she said and turned, walking away from him.

Once she got into her car and drove off, Jake remained on the porch, thinking. By the time he returned inside, several minutes had passed. He headed for the front living room, hearing voices and the animated laughter of his son. Everyone was there, including Hank, who had arrived with armloads of gifts, even though he was on call over the holidays. Ellie was hanging a few fallen ornaments back onto the Christmas tree, and the kids were playing a game by the window. Mitch and Tess were sitting close together on the couch. Grant had arrived the night before and was on the other couch, working on his laptop, but still very present. Joss had returned from the kitchen with a tray of food provided by Mrs. B—everything was as it should be. *His family.* And yet Jake experienced an acute sense of disconnection as he looked around the room.

T.J. looked happy and distracted, enjoying the games with his cousins, clearly oblivious to the chaos surrounding him. A surge of love washed over Jake like a wave. He loved him as Abby loved him—with his whole heart.

I love him so much because he's your son...

Something uncurled in his chest. A realization. Mixed with memory. About Abby. About everything they had been to one another. Since high school. Since he'd returned to Cedar River. He remembered how she'd acted when they had met again, how she'd asked him to meet her at the Loose Moose. How they had talked over and over, time after time, and not once did she try to mention T.J. was his son. Or did she? She'd said they needed to talk after the wedding, but he'd been so wrapped up being with her, so mesmerized by the reality of having her back in his arms, he hadn't listened.

"Hey, Jake," Joss said cheerfully. "Where's Abby? I thought she might have stayed for a while."

"Mommy's gone home," T.J. said, clearly hearing everything.

Joss frowned and looked at Jake. "She's alone today?"

Discomfort pressed down on his shoulders. "I don't—"

"Great-Gran has gone to see my grandma," T.J. announced. "But Mommy stayed at home."

Jake felt several pairs of eyes jerk in his direction, and he held up his hands. "She said she was working."

Joss and Mitch were both shaking their heads. "What?"

"Exactly," Mitch said with an exasperated breath. "What are you doing?"

Jake laughed humorlessly. "The truth? I don't have a clue."

"Well, at least you're capable of admitting it," Hank said and grinned.

Jake propped his hands on his hips. "Okay...so I'm admitting I'm an idiot who doesn't know what to do about the—"

"About the fact you're still in love with Abby?" Joss said and laughed.

"I know you might all believe it's simple math that Abby and I should…you know," he said and made sure his son wasn't listening too closely. "But it's too complicated." He let out a long breath. "It's crazy…impossible…but…"

"But?" Mitch persisted.

Jake tried to think of something to say, some way to dig himself out of the humiliating hole he was in. And came up with nothing. All he could think about, were Abby's parting words.

I love him so much because he's your son…

There had been such raw emotion in her voice…such… *truth*.

And then Jake realized how blind he'd been since he'd returned to town. He'd been bent on building bridges, seeking Abby's forgiveness for the way they'll parted years earlier. But in his determination to make things right, he hadn't seen what was right in front of him. His desire for her had given him blinders to what was really happening. The real truth. About his feelings for Abby and her feelings for him. And that blindness had made him angry and resentful, particularly since he'd discovered that T.J. was his son. Resentment that had come to define him. Resentment that had made him small and mean and not the best version of himself. Shame, gut wrenching and powerful, pressed down on his shoulders and surged through his blood. He'd made so many mistakes…things he wasn't sure he could undo.

"I think she still…" His words trailed off, and he felt his cheek grow hotter. "You know…"

"Loves you?" Joss teased, and his brothers all laughed. "Of course she does… What's not to love?"

Jake laughed at himself. "Oh, you know, the fact that

I'm closed off, uncommunicative and terrified of intimacy."

"Yeah," Mitch said and smiled. "But we all know that, and we *still* love you."

His throat tightened. "I…you know…feel the same… about all of you."

Mitch laughed. "We know. So…what are you gonna do about the mother of your child?"

Jake looked at his brothers, sister and sister-in-law, saw their smiles and nods of approval, and knew it was time he stopped denying the obvious. He loved Abby. He always had. And he wanted her to be more than the mother of his son.

"Hey, buddy," he said to T.J. and beckoned him. "I've gotta go out for a while. Can you stay here with your uncle Mitch and aunt Tess?"

"Where are you going, Daddy?"

He picked him up and hugged him close. "I have to go and tell your mommy that I can't live without her. Is that okay?"

T.J. laughed delightedly. "That's okay, Daddy. 'Cause I can't live without her, either."

"I know, buddy," he said and kissed his son's forehead. "Be a good boy. I'll be back soon." He glanced at his brother. "Okay?"

Mitch nodded and grinned. "Get outta here."

Jake pulled his keys from his pocket, hugged his son once more and left the room.

Abby stared at the gifts beneath the tree. Gifts she would be opening with her son the following day. Gifts from her grandmother, from her friend Renee, from her mother and step-dad. The tree sparkled, mocking her misery, and she fought the tears burning behind her eyes.

Don't be foolish.

She knew shouldn't feel so wretchedly alone, but she did. Without T.J., the house seemed so empty, and she didn't like the feeling. Her son's laughter usually echoed around the rooms, the sound of his footsteps a constant reminder of how much love and joy he brought to her life. Without him, nothing seemed right.

You knew it would be like this.

Of course she did. And she could not have denied her son the chance to spend the holidays with his dad. She knew how much he adored Jake, and she was genuinely happy he was forging a strong and loving relationship with his father. But she *missed* him profoundly. And she missed the way things used to be. She missed being the center of his universe and the person he relied on the most. And she missed other things, too. She missed Jake's company. Since he'd come back, in those few weeks, Abby had become accustomed to seeing him. And for a while, things between them had been good. Almost as though they were rekindling what they'd once had. The way he'd kindly agreed to teach T.J. to snowboard before he even knew he was his son, or how he'd helped them find a Christmas tree—those things had made it seem as though they had truly reconnected. And, of course, after the wedding they'd made love, and it had been incredible.

But then Jake discovered the truth about T.J., and everything changed. His time. His touch. His intentions.

Like she'd known they would.

In the past couple of weeks, she'd come close to telling him she loved him so many times. Even today, at the ranch, she'd skirted around the words. Because she was scared of his response…of his rejection.

She bit back a sob and was about to head to the kitchen to make tea when she heard a sharp knock on the front door. She wasn't expecting anyone. The only person likely to drop by unannounced was Annie, and she knew her friend was spending the afternoon with David McCall and his family before they headed to the Triple C to celebrate Christmas with the Culhanes.

Abby walked down the hall and pulled the door back on its hinges and discovered Jake standing on the other side of the screen. "Jake!" she exclaimed and looked around the porch. "What's wrong? Where's T.J.?"

"He's fine," he replied. "He's at the ranch with Mitch and Tess."

"What are you doing here?"

"I need to talk to you," he replied. "Can I come in?"

She opened the screen. "Of course."

Moments later they were in the living room. Jake ditched his jacket and stood by the fireplace, his expression unreadable. He watched her with scorching intensity, his gaze unwavering.

"I went to the hotel," he said, one brow up a fraction. "I was told it was your day off."

She managed a painful shrug. "I just said that I was working to, you know…make things easier. I didn't want to intrude on your family."

"My family?" he echoed and nodded, looking at her intensely. "Yeah…that's why I'm here—to talk about *my* family." He exhaled heavily. "So, turns out I have this problem."

"Problem?" she queried, her chest tightening.

He nodded. "Yes, a problem. The thing is, I'm really mad at you."

Abby shook her head. "I know, Jake. Did you really come all this way on Christmas Eve to tell me that?"

He shrugged, dropping his broad shoulders. "You see,

I know that my being mad hurts you," he said quietly and then winced, breathing hard. "And that just kills me."

She stilled. "Jake... I..."

"So," he said, his voice the only thing she heard above the wild pounding of her heart, "I have to forgive you. I have to forgive you and forget that I'm angry and bitter and somehow let go of all those feelings."

"Why?" she asked, not daring to let herself believe what she was hearing.

"Because," he said, his hands dropping "when you're in love with someone, you have to forgive them. Otherwise, what's the point? Do you agree?"

She nodded, unsure where the conversation was heading. "I...yes."

"And I love you, Abby. I've loved you since we were sixteen."

Abby's heart clenched behind her ribs, and she shuddered. "I love you, too."

He nodded, and his eyes had never glittered more brilliantly. "I know...after what you said to me at the ranch... I know."

"I never wanted him to be anyone's child but yours," she admitted, tears filling her eyes.

He was in front of her in three strides, grabbing her hands and holding them against his chest. "Abby, we've wasted so much time on bitterness and anger...let's not do that anymore," he said softly, clutching her hands. "I want to start over...you and me. Do you think you might want to do that?"

Abby nodded. "I want that more than anything."

He claimed her lips with a kiss that was so sweet that she sighed against his mouth, clutching him, feeling his warmth and strength seep through to her bones.

"Let's sit down," he said raggedly and led her to the sofa.

Abby curled against him, so happy she could barely speak. But she knew she had to. There were things that needed to be said. Wounds that needed to healed.

"I want to say something," she said and placed two fingers gently against his mouth. "And I'd like to say them without you interrupting me." He nodded and she continued. "I'm sorry, Jake, for everything."

"Abby, I—"

She shushed him and touched his mouth again. "Please… I need to say this."

He swallowed hard. "Okay."

Abby grabbed his hand, holding it tightly. "Back then, I didn't understand why you needed to join the military. I'm sorry I didn't realize how much it had to do with your father leaving and your mom dying. I'm sorry I was bullheaded and unforgiving at the time."

"We were young," he said. "And both of us were bullheaded."

"Maybe," she said agreeably. "But at least you stood by your principles. I was so wrapped up in punishing you I couldn't think straight."

"I had to go," he said quietly. "I had to get the shadow of Billie-Jack off my tail."

"I know that, *now*," she said and shuddered with emotion.

"And I understand, Abby," he said gently. "I get why you didn't want to be with a soldier. I know you were scared."

"I was terrified of losing you," she admitted. "And of ending up as unhappy as my mom."

"I didn't mean for you to have to make a choice," he said, swallowing hard. "I should have been more understanding. I knew about your mom and dad, I knew what you were feeling back then. The truth is, I should have fought harder for us. I didn't because, like you, I was afraid of ending up like my parent. I guess we're not so different, after all."

She nodded, hearing the real emotion in his voice. "Jake, I'm sorry I married Tom. He deserved more than what I was able to give him. And so did you. I loved him, and I cared about him deeply, but I was never *in* love with him. My heart has always belonged to you," she stated, fighting back tears. "And it always will.

"Mine, too, sweetheart," he said and gently kissed her knuckles. "And don't be sorry for marrying Tom…he was a good guy. I'm not going to deny that it didn't hurt, but you know, marrying him wasn't a mistake. He died when he was twenty-five, which is way too young, but I'm willing to bet you gave him so much happiness every day that you were together."

Abby's love for him intensified. "Tom once told me you were the most honorable and decent man he knew," she said softly. "And he was right. You are. But there's something else I need to say."

"I'm listening."

Abby rested a hand against his cheek. "I'm sorry I denied you the chance to be T.J.'s father…because you are incredible at it," she said and rubbed her thumb along his jaw. "I am so humbled by the way you love him, Jake."

"He's easy to love," Jake said gently. "I am so proud to be his dad. I want to give him the world, Abby," he said, taking her hand and interlinking their fingers. "And you. I want to give you everything. I want to love you and cherish you and…" He paused, taking a breath. "Marry you… if you'll have me."

"Are you proposing?" Abby managed to ask, her heart almost bursting.

"I certainly am," he said and turned over her hand. "Although I need to get a ring. I mean, I'd thought about it, but I never..." His words trailed off and he dropped her hand and quickly got to his feet. He walked to where his jacket lay on the back of a chair and pulled a small parcel from the pocket. He came back to the sofa and sat down, fumbling with the parcel a little. "I have this," he said and shook the gift wrapped in Christmas paper.

"What is it?" she asked.

"Open it and see," he suggested and smiled, his handsome face melting her.

Abby took the parcel and unwrapped it, revealing a narrow velvet box. She flipped the lid and found a beautiful gold and diamond necklace. "It's so lovely."

"A Christmas gift. But I didn't know how to give it to you." He took out the pendant and turned it over. "I had it engraved."

Abby read the inscription. "'A. For always. In all ways. J.'"

The tears she'd been battling to keep at bay tumbled down her cheeks. "Oh...that's so—"

"Marry me, Abby?" he asked quickly. "Please?"

She nodded. "Yes, Jake, there's nothing I want more than to marry you."

He reached around and clipped the necklace around her throat. "Until we get a ring."

"It has diamonds," she said happily, still crying. "That's good enough."

He kissed her passionately, and Abby was filled with so much love she could barely breathe. When he pulled back, he gently wiped her cheeks with his thumb, staring deep into her eyes.

"No more tears, okay?"

She nodded. "I promise. Except for happy tears."

"Those are okay," he said and kissed her again. "Tell me you don't want a long engagement?"

Abby smiled against his mouth. "Definitely not. As soon as the law allows."

"And the house by the river, do you think you'd be happy there?"

She sighed dreamily. "Absolutely."

"Even though it would mean moving away from your grandmother?"

"Gran won't mind," she said and sighed. "You know, she's always referred to you as my *quicksand*. She's right," she said and grasped his shoulders. "You are. I love you, Jake. You're the love of my life. Marrying you, raising our son with you, that's all I want."

He held her gently. "Me, too. So how about we go back to the ranch and tell our son that we're getting married?"

She nodded. "I think that's a great idea."

He took her hands and gently urged her to her feet, holding her close. "Then let's go, future Mrs. Culhane."

Abby had never heard sweeter words and realized she had everything she'd ever wanted. And more. A beautiful son and the love of the one man who filled her heart. *Her* family.

Epilogue

The last place that anyone expected to be on Christmas Day was the Cedar River Community Hospital. But that's where every Culhane was, taking turns to visit the newest family member—Mitch and Tess's newborn son. His sister-in-law had gone into an early labor late on Christmas Eve, nearly two weeks before her due date. He was glad that Abby had been at this side and knew she was remembering her own experience when their son was born.

It had been a whirlwind twenty-four hours. And Jake had never been happier.

The family had embraced the news of his engagement to Abby, and T.J. was clearly ecstatic at the prospect of his parents getting married. They'd spent the night at the ranch and no one said anything about the fact that Abby had spent it with him. Having her in his arms, making love to her, was like having every dream come true. They'd spent the evening celebrating, sharing dinner with his family, watching the kids play, while Joss had played Christmas tunes on the piano. It was close to ten o'clock when Mitch took Tess to the hospital. And a few hours later, the little boy was born.

"He's so beautiful," Abby said as they admired the newest Culhane.

Although he was born early, the baby was completely healthy. However, he was put in a special incubator first to ensure his lungs were working to capacity. But after twelve hours, he was given the all clear. Now they were in Tess's hospital room, and the new mom was holding the infant, while Mitch was looking on proudly. Jake felt such happiness for his brother—he and Tess had gone through so much to get to where they were—through grief and heartache, and then forgiveness. Much like he had with Abby.

"We think so," Mitch said, clearly enamored with his new son.

Jake grasped Abby's hand, linking their fingers. She looked so beautiful she made him breathless. "Congratulations."

Mitch grinned. "To you both, as well, on your engagement," he said, looking incredibly sentimental. "Who would have thought just a few short months ago that we'd both be back with the only women we've ever loved, and have kids?"

Jake laughed softly. "Not me. But I think things have turned out exactly the way they were supposed to."

The truth of his own words made *him* feel sentimental. So much had changed. He'd come home to support his brother after the accident, and although he'd wanted to mend fences with Abby, the notion of romantically reconnecting with her felt about as far removed as the stars from some distant planet. But now, as he held her hand in his, as he felt her pressed against him and could pick up the familiar sent of her fragrance, Jake marveled at how his life had done such a complete 180.

"So, when's the wedding?" Tess asked.

"Soon," Jake replied and squeezed Abby's hand. "Or if our son has his way, today."

Abby laughed, and the sound hit him squarely in the chest. "There's enough excitement happening today. But yes, it will definitely be soon."

They stayed a little while longer, and he was utterly mesmerized by the baby, by Mitch and Tess's happiness, by the way Abby gripped his hand, holding on, giving him strength and taking, too. It was, he figured, exactly what it should be.

When they left the room, T.J. came bounding down the corridor. He'd been hanging with Ellie in the visitors' lounge and was clearly delighted to see them.

"Mommy, Mommy," he asked and hugged his mother. "Did you see the baby?"

"I did," she replied and grabbed his hand. "He's beautiful."

Their son looked at them quizzically. "Boys aren't beautiful, Mommy...they're handsome."

"He's right," Jake said and grinned. "Baby *girls* are beautiful. Speaking of which," he added, once they'd said goodbye to Ellie and headed out, "we should make one of those."

Abby stopped walking beside him. "What?"

"A girl," he replied and grabbed her hand, keeping her moving and leading her toward the entrance. "Or another boy. We make cute kids," he said and gestured toward their son, who was a few paces in front of them. "Another one would be good."

She raised a brow. "You want to have a baby?"

He nodded, loving her so much he could barely breathe. "I do."

"You know what that means?" She smiled warmly. "Late nights. Little sleep...sometimes *no* sleep. Diapers. Vomit. Croup. Endless laundry."

"Sounds like fun."

She laughed. "My, how you've changed."

"You changed me," he acknowledged as they walked through the doors. He called T.J. back, and their son quickly rushed to his side. "I used to avoid commitment like the plague. But now, it's all I want."

Abby reached up and touched his face. "Merry Christmas, Jake."

"Merry Christmas, sweetheart," he said and kissed her softly.

T.J. giggled. "Daddy, are you going to kiss Mommy every day from now on?"

"You bet, buddy."

Their son moved between them and grabbed their hands, and they swung him gently in the air as they walked across the parking lot and toward his Jeep, his laughter like music to their ears. Jake marveled at how lucky he was. He had the woman he loved and his son at his side, and he knew, without doubt or fear or any lingering resentment, that he had everything he could ever want.

It was a perfect moment.

And he had a whole lifetime of moments just like it to look forward to.

How he'd gotten so lucky, Jake wasn't sure, but he knew he'd be forever grateful for all they had and everything that lay ahead. A home. Marriage. More children. And a love that made him a better man.

"What are you thinking about?" Abby asked as they playfully swung their laughing son between them again.

Jake smiled, loving her, loving the little boy who'd brought them back together.

"The future."

* * * * *

Don't miss Annie's story,
the next installment in Helen Lacey's miniseries
The Culhanes Of Cedar River,
Coming in 2020.

And look for Mitch and Tess's story,
When You Least Expect It

Available now wherever Harlequin books
and ebooks are sold.

WE HOPE YOU ENJOYED THIS BOOK!

HARLEQUIN®

SPECIAL EDITION

Open your heart to more true-to-life stories of love and family.

Discover six new books available every month, wherever books are sold.

HSEHALO0419

COMING NEXT MONTH FROM

H HARLEQUIN®

SPECIAL EDITION

Available December 17, 2019

#2737 FORTUNE'S FRESH START
The Fortunes of Texas: Rambling Rose • by Michelle Major
In the small Texas burg of Rambling Rose, real estate investor Callum Fortune is making a big splash. The last thing he needs is any personal complications slowing his pace—least of all nurse Becky Averill, a beautiful widow with twin baby girls!

#2738 HER RIGHT-HAND COWBOY
Forever, Texas • by Marie Ferrarella
A clause in her father's will requires Ena O'Rourke to work the family ranch for six months before she can sell it. She's livid at her father throwing a wrench in her life from beyond the grave. But Mitch Randall, foreman of the Double E, is always there for her. As Ena spends more time on the ranch—and with Mitch—new memories are laid over the old...and perhaps new opportunities to make a life.

#2739 SECOND-CHANCE SWEET SHOP
Wickham Falls Weddings • by Rochelle Alers
Brand-new bakery owner Sasha Manning didn't anticipate that the teenager she hired would have a father more delectable than anything in her shop window! Sasha still smarts from falling for a man too good to be true. Divorced single dad Dwight Adams will have to prove to Sasha that he's the real deal and not a wolf in sheep's clothing...and learn to trust someone with his heart along the way.

#2740 COOKING UP ROMANCE
The Taylor Triplets • by Lynne Marshall
Lacy was a redhead with a pink food truck who prepared mouthwatering meals. Hunky construction manager Zack Gardner agreed to let her feed his hungry crew in exchange for cooking lessons for his young daughter. But it looked like the lovely businesswoman was transforming the single dad's life in more ways than one—since a family secret is going to change both of their lives in ways they never expected.

#2741 RELUCTANT HOMETOWN HERO
Wildfire Ridge • by Heatherly Bell
Former army officer Ryan Davis doesn't relish the high-profile role of town sheriff, but when duty calls, he responds. Even if it means helping animal rescuer Zoey Castillo find her missing foster dog. When Ryan asks her out, Zoey is wary of a relationship in the spotlight—especially given her past. If the sheriff wants to date her, he'll have to prove that two legs are better than four.

#2742 THE WEDDING TRUCE
Something True • by Kerri Carpenter
For the sake of their best friends' wedding, divorce attorney Xander Ryan and wedding planner Grace Harris are calling a truce. Now they must plan the perfect wedding shower together. But Xander doesn't believe in marriage! And Grace believes in romance and true love. Clearly, they have nothing in common. In fact, all Xander feels when Grace is near is disdain and...desire. Wait. What?

YOU CAN FIND MORE INFORMATION ON UPCOMING HARLEQUIN® TITLES, FREE EXCERPTS AND MORE AT WWW.HARLEQUIN.COM.

HSECNM1219

Love Harlequin romance?

DISCOVER.

Be the first to find out about promotions, news and exclusive content!

 Facebook.com/HarlequinBooks

 Twitter.com/HarlequinBooks

Instagram.com/HarlequinBooks

Pinterest.com/HarlequinBooks

ReaderService.com

EXPLORE.

Sign up for the Harlequin e-newsletter and download a free book from any series at **TryHarlequin.com.**

CONNECT.

Join our Harlequin community to share your thoughts and connect with other romance readers!
Facebook.com/groups/HarlequinConnection

HARLEQUIN®

ROMANCE WHEN
YOU NEED IT